THE FOUR HORSEMEN: DESCENT

L J SWALLOW

Copyright © 2018 by L J Swallow

All rights reserved.

No part of this book may be reproduced in any form or by any electronic or mechanical means, including information storage and retrieval systems, without written permission from the author, except for the use of brief quotations in a book review.

1

Joss

I check my phone for the third time, pissed off that I've been left alone in a crowded room filled with people I don't want to talk to. Sure, somebody needs to hang around and watch, but Ewan left to check on Vee a long time ago and hasn't returned.

I rest against the wall. I bet Ewan's taken Vee back to their room. All evening, I've sensed his distraction, and I don't need three guesses what he and Vee are doing right now. Either that or Ewan's finally decided to punch Seth, and they're dealing with the aftermath.

Interesting times ahead if he has, either way.

As each minute passes, the room empties further as the alcohol dries up and people leave. I watch as the crowd dwindles to a couple of drunken businesspeople whose raucous laughter grates on my nerves.

Screw this.

I drain my wine glass and set it on the nearby table, beside empty plates covered in half-eaten pastry parcels.

I didn't think it could get much colder, but I rub my arms as I step into the icy world and the temperature drops. No wonder the trio aren't out here. I check my phone—over an hour since they left. Ewan could've bloody let me know what was happening instead of leaving me in the party like an abandoned puppy.

But I guess I wasn't on Ewan's mind. Two people pass and head towards the coach house. I pause. Where are Heath and Xander? They disappeared an hour ago too. I check my phone. Nothing. From any of them.

Should I be worried? In situations like this, we rendezvous at wherever we're using as a base. Heath and Xander can easily look after themselves; I'll head back, and if Ewan is getting down and dirty with Vee, I'll wait for the brothers to arrive back.

I hurry down the pathway, and when I reach the building, the main door is open and snow blows into the hallway. Frowning, I step inside and adjust my eyes to the bright hallway light.

Ewan sits on the floor, back against the wall. He doesn't notice me as his head is tilted upwards and eyes closed. What the fuck? Ewan's clutching his stomach and his eyes fly open as I touch him on the shoulder.

"Ewan?"

He's pale, face twisted in pain as he looks up at me.

"Vee. Did you see Vee?" he asks in a hoarse voice.

"No. What the fuck happened?" I look around, wild-eyed, terrified in case one of the things that attacked him before are around. I crouch down and touch Ewan's perspiring forehead.

He's clammy and cool. "Who attacked you?"

"Seth."

I reel. "How? Shit. Did he hurt Vee too?"

I stand again, and Ewan shakes his head and attempts to pull himself upright. Instead, he winces and slumps back down. "I don't know what the fuck he is, but Seth isn't human. He just beat the crap out of me and then..." Ewan waves a hand. "Disappeared."

"With Vee?" I ready myself to rush out the door and find them. I'm prepared to risk my chances against Seth and get more answers from Ewan later.

"No. Teleported or some shit." Ewan pushes both hands into his hair. "I don't know what happened, Joss."

"Vee?" I ask urgently. "Did he hurt Vee?"

"No. That's a whole other issue." He regards me through tired eyes. "We... yeah." He pauses, and I nod to show I know what he means. "It happened, and afterwards she just turned fucking weird. Totally freaked out like she was in pain or something. Vee left."

"Where?"

"I don't know. I couldn't catch up because Seth caught me first." He swallows. "I'll be okay, but Vee...she was different, Joss. I'm worried, in case he's looking for her too."

I slide down the wall and onto the floor next to him. "How long ago?"

"Five minutes. Maybe ten. After Seth left, I was gonna leave, but can't walk properly." He holds up his phone. "I was about to text you."

I take a huge breath. It takes a hell of a lot to weaken any of us, especially Ewan, because his human form is bulkier. "Tell me everything that happened. I'll text Xander and find out what the hell he and Heath are up to."

I listen to Ewan's story and try to piece together the

scene in my head. There are more questions than I have answers to here, each word he says confuses me further. I'm pissed off—Seth's a supernatural creature, and I had no clue? I also have no idea how someone can switch from the weak person Seth is to something stronger, and that worries me. When demons possess, they're limited by their vessel's physical strengths and rely on any magic skills they have. I stitched Seth's arm. I sensed his weakness and uncertainty. We saw him assaulted and threatened. If Seth isn't a demon, what the fuck is he? No fae could do this.

"Are you sure it was Seth?" I ask Ewan.

"Yes. Unless someone replaced Seth while I was with Vee—not likely. I told you, the bastard has played us for days—weeks, even." Ewan attempts to stand again. "I've told you what I know. Now we find Vee, before he does."

He's right. It's less than five minutes since I found Ewan, but five minutes too long. I haul myself back to my feet. "Are you okay to wait here? I'll look for her."

He nods and waves a hand, clutching his stomach. "Yes. Go. I'll slow you down. If anything happens to Vee..." Ewan trails off.

"This is Vee he's messing with. A different Vee, too, if what you say is true. There's a reason Seth hasn't acted before now, and we need to find out why.

"Stop talking and just fucking look for her," he growls.

The door at the end of the hallway slams closed and my heart moves to my mouth. Seth? I ready myself, although fuck knows what I can do if it is him.

I jerk my head around and see Heath and Xander striding towards us. Xander passes by, staring ahead with a black look, and bangs open each bedroom door before turning to us.

"Where's Seth? Where's Vee?" His eyes are wide, and I sense his panic.

"They've both left," Ewan replies.

Xander storms over and leans down into Ewan's face. "What do you mean gone?"

"Vee left, Seth disappeared." He pauses. "Vanished."

"I told you," says Heath in a low voice. "He's Chaos."

I frown. "What do you mean?"

"I think he means we're fucking stupid." Ewan tips his head back and stares at the low ceiling. "I'm fucking stupid."

Xander spins on his heel and half runs to the door. "We find Vee. Now. I'll explain later."

Ewan meets my eyes, sharing my confusion.

Chaos?

---

*W*e all want to look for Vee, and Ewan tried to walk out with us, trying to convince us he was okay, but after taking a few steps he stumbled, the pain in his face clear.

Ewan shakes his head at me. He doesn't want me to tell the others how he feels. I wouldn't be able to, though, because what's behind Ewan's pain isn't only physical. He's a mess of emotion: confusion and fear. Guilt too? What exactly happened between him and Vee?

"I think Heath should stay with Ewan," I call after Xander. "Just in case."

Xander pauses and turns. Is he thinking the same as I am? I don't know how badly injured Ewan is, and he could need Heath.

Fuck. I rub my temples, annoyed the thought crossed my mind.

"Seth didn't do much. I'm okay. I'll be fine in five minutes." Typical Ewan, playing things down.

"I don't want to wait five minutes," snaps Xander. "Vee's been away too long already. We need to find her."

Ewan takes a shaky breath. "I tried to stop her. I'm sorry, okay?"

"Nobody's going to blame you for anything, Ewan." I reach out to touch his shoulder, but he flinches away.

"Come on!" urges Heath. "Stop wasting time."

"Exactly. We find Vee and then we need to talk about Logan and Ripley."

I jerk my head around to look at Xander from where I'm watching Ewan's face. "Ripley?"

"Yeah. Long story. It'll wait."

Heath interrupts, "He's here. Ripley told us about Chaos...Seth. We thought we were coming back here to find you and explain, and not find...this."

"Vee." Xander's voice is firm, tinged with fear. "We look for Vee before we do anything. I don't want to waste time swapping stories. Heath—stay here. Joss, come with me."

Xander and me leave them and rush out into the cold. The moon shines off the snow and lights our way between the coach house and the main building. Xander doesn't speak, but I'm as lost in my thoughts as he is.

Where would Vee go? What's happened to her?

Will she reject or accept us?

And what the hell did Heath mean about Ripley? Is he here?

Halfway to the house, I spot a female figure standing between two tall pine trees, at the edge of the area the cars are parked. I know in a heartbeat who this is; I push Xander's arm and point.

"Is she leaving?" I hiss.

"I hope she doesn't have car keys," Xander speaks the words as he picks up his pace and heads across the car park towards Vee. I shiver with the cold and fear. Is Vee still the girl we love?

She's facing away from us and staring across the grounds, standing tall, hands in her pockets. We stop short of Vee as if she's a wild animal we might scare away into the darkness she's looking into.

"Vee."

She turns her head at my voice, and I'm relieved to see her face is no different. What did I expect? A transformation into something harsher?

"I need to find someone, but I don't know what I'm looking for," she says in a flat voice, and turns back to stare across the grounds again. "There are powerful demons in the house. We should start with them."

"Start what?" asks Xander.

Vee turns to look at him, expression curious. "Killing them."

Xander swears under his breath. "We can't kill those demons, Vee. Not yet."

"Why?" Her voice hardens. "What if something is hiding amongst them?"

If only she understood the irony in her words. I step forward and reach out to take her hand. "We need to talk, Vee. Will you come back to the rooms?"

She folds her arms across her chest. "I don't have time. We don't have time. We kill those demons, and then we find more. We keep going until we find whoever I saw."

Xander straightens. "Who did you see? Where?"

Vee places fingertips on the side of her head. "I saw the world burning, Xander. Everything destroyed."

I didn't think my heart could beat any faster, but each

minute that passes since I saw Ewan terrifies me more. "What else did you see?" I ask.

Vee's breath mists around her head as her breathing quickens and she shakes her head. "Too much. But I know now. I know I have to stop him."

"Did you see Seth?"

"Why would I see Seth? He can't help."

"Please, come with us, and we'll explain." Xander steps forward too, and we're both wound tight, ready to stop Vee in case she decides to run.

Vee steps away. "You can stay or come with me. I'm going into that house and ending them. How many did you see? I know you saw more than Breanna. I can sense them." She sucks in a breath. "I'll end Logan too. I don't give a fuck who he is."

I've witnessed a vengeful Vee before, seen her shut down emotions and attack, and my greatest fear sneaks in. Has Ewan been the one to erase the humanity she once asked to lose?

"We need to talk," I repeat. "A lot has happened tonight."

"Like this. What happened to you?" asks Xander bluntly.

She blinks. "Didn't Ewan say? He was right. Once we had sex, he changed me, and now I know what I need to do. I know I'm strong enough."

For what? Rampaging through the world, taking down demons?

"How about we head back to Heath and Ewan," I say in a cajoling voice. "Ewan's worried about you."

She waves a hand. "Then where is he?"

I look at Xander who nods. "He's hurt, Vee."

"What? Was it me? Did I hurt him?" Her demeanour switches and I'm relieved the emotional connection remains enough to distract her from her plans. "Please tell me what happened to me didn't hurt him too."

"No. Seth did."

"Seth?" She frowns. "How? Did they fight? Did he have a weapon or something?"

I sigh and hold out a hand. "Let's talk somewhere warmer. All together, the way we should be."

Vee looks down at my hand, and as she hesitantly takes hold, my body floods with her emotions. This is like the day in the hall when I picked up on her distress, and the intensity is now turned up to maximum. But this isn't distress—it's a strength and determination I've never felt before.

"Your hands are hot for someone standing in the freezing Scottish countryside." I laugh, but she pulls away her hand again.

"Why are you so scared of me?" she whispers.

In a sudden move, Xander steps forward, and without looking at me, he seizes hold of Vee and pulls her to him. Vee's arms remain by her side as Xander envelops her in his arms. He rests his face against hers as he holds Vee tight.

I knew from Xander's few words how much he worried about what happened to Vee, but I never expected the guy who keeps his emotions in check to react to Vee physically. He doesn't let her go, and slowly she wraps her arms around his waist. They stand, together, beneath the moonlight in an embrace that relieves me but hurts at the same time.

I walk over and stroke Vee's hair. She trembles as she moves and rests her head against Xander's chest.

I touch Vee's cheek and her skin burns against my hand, like a patient with a fever who should be delirious at this temperature. "You're burning up, Vee."

"Yeah, holding you is like holding fire." Xander moves his head to look at her. "The same as always."

Vee smiles, filling my heart with more relief, until she speaks. "I'll talk to you. Then you need to let me go."

In response, Xander's hold on her tightens. I wait for him to argue, to tell her no, but perhaps he understands how much of Vee's War has been triggered by whatever happened.

He looks at me. There's no way in hell we're letting Vee out of sight.

2

XANDER

Vee walks back to the coach house with us; I half expected her to veer off to the house and seek out the demons she's determined to kill, but she doesn't. I'm not Joss, but when I held her, I sensed myself—War—in her, stronger than ever.

The moment Ewan told me Vee had disappeared, my world flipped. What if I never saw her again? All this time and I'd never shown her how she'd changed me; how she strengthened me by weakening my walls. I never told her the truth.

Holding her in my arms brought relief despite her initial stiffness, but the tighter I held Vee, the more the girl inside yielded. I whispered to Vee that she shouldn't give in to the intense need to attack. I told her to stay calm and weigh things up.

Vee smiled and whispered back that I was a hypocrite, and my heart stopped hurting.

At that moment, I knew she was still our Vee.

Vee forges ahead and pushes through the door at the coach house, which slams hard against the wall. Immediately she's with Ewan, kneeling down and touching him. She takes his hand, and my last doubts Vee might have lost who she is leave.

Ewan and Vee embrace as tightly as we did before. She pushes his hair from his face, kisses him, holds his cheeks, and they talk in low, urgent tones. I hang back with Joss, and Heath walks to us.

"How is she?" asks Heath.

"Herself, but not," replies Joss. "She seems stronger, more focused, but there's something more. Did you feel it, Xander?"

"There's a different energy to her," I reply in a low voice so she can't hear. "And I honestly think if she leaves us, she'll storm through the house and kill every demon she can find. Right now, that isn't helpful."

"Did you tell her about Seth?" asks Heath. "I filled Ewan in."

"No. We haven't had a chance." I tip my head to where she stands with Ewan. "I'm worried she might lose her shit and disappear to look for him."

"I'd like someone to tell me about Seth. And Ripley," Joss puts in. "What do you mean he's Chaos?"

I give Joss a staccato version of events, one eye still on Vee, and through his shock, he tells me what happened to Ewan. None of us has the full facts on any of this, and we need to sit and straighten all this out before we can decide on our next move.

"Vee doesn't know who he is, not even after she changed

or whatever happened, so how can she find him?"

"Maybe he's not the person she saw in her vision," replies Joss.

Heath straightens. "What vision?"

"We're not sure. Hopefully, she'll explain more."

"Then how the hell do we find Seth?" asks Joss.

"I think we'll need to wait until he's ready for us to find him." Heath rubs his cheek. "Or until he finds us first. I honestly think Seth wants to have fun with us before he unleashes whatever hell he's planning."

"If Ripley is telling the truth."

I did doubt Ripley—until I came back here and saw the aftermath. Another big doubt ebbs too—Vee must be here to help us, otherwise she would fight with and undermine us the way Seth did. Or she would've left with him.

Vee stands and straightens her clothes before approaching. Her pink cheeks and hard expression are matched by a harsh voice. "Ewan told me what happened. About Seth. Chaos. I feel so fucking stupid, because this is my fault." I blink at her vehemence. "I brought Seth to us. I persuaded you to keep him there."

Joss holds her face in both hands and his eyes search hers. "Vee, you've always known when people lie. Of course you'd trust someone you couldn't detect told lies to you."

"But how?" she says. "Why didn't I know he lied?"

"He's a dangerous god, Vee. We don't know what he's capable of."

She looks past Joss to me. "I need to meet this Ripley. And I have a few choice words for Logan."

I wipe a hand down my face. The biggest vibe I'm getting from Vee is that she's likely to do what drives her and not listen to anybody—including me.

"I think we need to sit down calmly and talk."

Ewan stands, more colour in his face, unable to keep his eyes off Vee. Is he wary of her? "I'm okay. I agree with Vee. I want to meet Ripley, but I don't trust him either."

"We'll speak to them tomorrow. I don't think there's much we can do right now. We agreed to speak to Ripley and his gang in the morning, and there's no sign of Seth. I say we need to sleep and hope he doesn't come back to try to take on five of us."

Vee shakes her head. "I'm not tired. I want to look for Seth."

"How?" I ask as gently as I can.

"He's looking for me. Ewan said I have something he needs. I doubt I'll manage to go far alone before he finds me."

Ewan takes Vee's hand. "No. We work together. Don't put yourself in danger."

"He's right. Everybody needs to stick together from now on. Look what happened to Ewan." Vee chews her bottom lip but doesn't respond to me. "We rest and can take turns on watch in case he does come back."

Heath rubs her arm. "We're stronger together. That's what he always tried to stop."

"Unity." Ewan squeezes her hand.

I indicate to Heath we should leave as Vee turns her attention to Ewan again. I hope he can persuade her to stay. They speak in low tones and walk into the bedroom they share.

"I think somebody needs to stay awake and watch Vee," I say to Joss as Ewan closes the bedroom door. "We've made too many mistakes recently."

Heath chuckles. "I don't think she'll be happy with that."

"Do you want her to disappear to god knows where? Or attack the people we need to work with?" I ask.

"She won't."

"You're very confident. Touch her. Get close. You'll feel she's different. She never listened to me before this, let alone now." I gesture at the door.

"Fine. But I doubt she'll sleep anyway if she's wired."

"Ewan will keep an eye on her." Heath crosses to open his bedroom door. "I imagine they have a lot to talk about."

Vee

I sit in the chair by the window in the room I share with Ewan, gazing out at the distant highlands. I need to be here, with the guys, but I also feel trapped.

They don't understand.

The guys haven't seen what I did.

But I can't tell them everything I saw. Not yet.

Understandably, they're cautious—even Xander. And what the hell is he doing, considering siding with their enemies? Trusting those who spent the last few years trying to kill them?

The way I trusted Seth.

I'm so fucking angry he tricked me. Ewan told me how he transformed, and as he described the scene everything made sense. The figure made up of a void in my vision was Seth.

But what I saw won't happen. I will stop the guys dying.

I will stop the end of the world.

The thoughts weave in and out, obsessive, spurring me towards action I don't know how to take yet. As the minutes pass, my human body tires and aches. Is the pain because I'm struggling to contain whatever hit me after sex with Ewan? Or is something slowly killing human me the way I've seen in movies when people become vampires?

One thing's for sure, my senses are sharper. I can hear what Xander is saying to Heath. He's concerned that I'll run. But I won't. Part of this has tightened the thread holding us, as individuals and as a whole. The Four are part of who I am, and I need them more than ever.

An exhausted-looking Ewan interrupts my thoughts as his large frame moves in front of the window. I look up, unblinking, and pick up on his mixture of concern and desire.

"We need to talk about what happened," Ewan says cautiously.

"The sex or my changing?"

"Both."

My breath catches, as looking into his darkened eyes triggers recent memories and a deep, low heat inside rises. My need for the guys hasn't left and intensifies as Ewan watches me.

"I think I hurt you," he says.

"No."

"You were terrified."

"But I'm okay now. You weren't responsible—I don't think we could've stopped it. I feel stronger."

"That worries me too."

I stand and reach out to trace his lips with my fingertips, the mouth that covered mine, that explored my body. "You're frightened I'll leave, aren't you?"

He holds my fingers and pulls them away. "You already did. You walked away from me afterwards. Are you hiding why?"

"Do you think I'm lying that I'll stay? I'm still Truth, and I still can't lie." I give a wry smile, but he doesn't return it. "Ewan. I belong with you all. How many times do I need to say this? Whatever has changed inside me connects us more."

"Then why did you walk away?"

"In that moment, I wasn't me, Ewan. I didn't know what the hell was happening to me." I attempt to explain exactly what happened but play down the fear and pain when Ewan's worry grows. "I'm okay now, though."

He shakes his head. "You say that like it was nothing. This is big. Xander is worried. We all are."

"It's only been a couple of hours." I tiptoe to place my lips on his. The need to stay with them all, to draw on the strength they give me, has intensified, not dropped.

But will they listen to me when I tell them what I need to do? Support me when I clash with Xander about our next move? Nobody knows what this is. I don't know yet, but I feel the pull to be something. Will this drag me away from the guys?

"Okay." Ewan wraps his arms around me and hugs me tightly against his hard chest. I breathe in the scent lingering after our sex: perspiration and his cologne that intoxicated me. "I love you, Vee. I don't want to lose you."

I want to tell Ewan that he won't lose me, but how can I guarantee anything when I don't understand what's happening to me? Ewan's heart beats faster when I don't respond, so I tell him with a gentle kiss that I'm here, his—theirs. That whatever happens, they always will be.

"I love you, Ewan. I'm sorry I walked away when I said I wouldn't. I didn't go far."

"You're back now, and you're with me. That's what matters." He holds my cheeks in his broad palms and kisses me softly and gently, pulling my heart further into his. As I wrap my arms around Ewan's waist, he winces.

"Are you okay?" I ask and touch his side gently.

"Tired. Big day." He kisses my forehead. "Maybe we should sleep."

"I can't. I'm too wired."

"Vee. It's 4 a.m. Today has been exhausting. If anything, gather your energy for our meeting with Ripley tomorrow."

Adrenaline surges instantly the moment the thought of demons enters my head. Will I be able to control my contained fury, and the overwhelming desire to kill them?

I know Ewan won't let me go, and I want his comfort, so I head to bed with him. I smile as he almost instantly falls asleep. He's shirtless, so I play my fingers from his smooth chest to his side and run the tips around the outline of his tattoos. I want to remind myself of him—and us. Despite the poor light, I can see the dark bruise Seth caused, spreading across his stomach.

Ewan winces and murmurs in his sleep when I lightly touch the dark skin. He healed quickly after the fight with the diseased creatures, surely a bruise should be gone by now? I place my palm against him, wishing he hadn't been hurt, blaming myself, as I watch his shallow breathing. If I'd stayed instead of running blindly through the door, would Seth still have revealed himself? Would I have stopped him hurting Ewan?

I lean forward to kiss Ewan's forehead and an electric energy interrupts, running from my heart to my wrist, downwards into the fingers touching his skin. In the dim, a slight glow around the tips shines back at me. As he mumbles again, I pull my hand away, terrified I could be hurting him.

Instead, Ewan's skin is now clear.

A new hope surges. If I can heal Ewan, does this mean I'm now capable of resurrecting the guys? Heart buoyed further, I settle my head against his chest and attempt to sleep.

As I drift into the welcome blackness of sleep, a thought follows me:

Am I really still Vee?

3

ANDER

I'm confused how Ripley finds time to impersonate Alasdair and run his conference while dealing with the bigger picture.

How long has he been 'Alasdair'?

Whatever, I'm bloody glad I don't have to sit through presentations on the Foundation's history and plans. Although, the new agenda in my life isn't much fun either: discuss how to work effectively with the demon who's usually hell-bent on killing us, and vice versa.

So we gather, wary, in the same meeting room as last night. I refuse to sit as I wait for Joss to arrive with Vee. She says she's okay, but there's something different in her eyes; a sharp response to any noise or suspicion about demons. Her repeated threat she'll kill them.

Joss is currently talking her down from storming in here and taking out Ripley. We've told her to listen first, and she wavers between accepting the situation and disagreeing, in the way I do.

Joss needs to stay by her side.

Joss and Ewan are more suspicious than I am, but then they never sat and heard the story. I also haven't mentioned what Breanna said about Joss; as if she's aware of something we're not. Her words tugged at my own fears—I don't want my visions any clearer.

Breanna sits here now, quietly, watching. I can't decide how close she's linked to Ripley. I sense she's her own person, because most demons I come across fawn over Ripley, or are scared for their lives if they say the wrong thing. I've tried hard to remember if I've seen Breanna before the way Joss says he has, but I can't find her in my memories.

Ripley sits beside her in the same place at the table, but is dressed down today—jeans and shirt. He wears a warm jacket. Planning a quick getaway? I refuse to hand over our knives as we walk in, and when he accepts this without question, I know the situation is really screwed.

Ewan remains by the door, arms crossed and face dark. He's okay this morning, his injury gone, so at least we know Seth's damage is as temporary as any other supe has managed. Or we hope so; we can't count on anything. Between us, we've agreed that as soon as the meeting is finished we're leaving for home and deciding where to go.

I'm convinced Seth's next move will be to attack a portal, if opening them is his ultimate plan. But which one?

Logan is here too, at a sensible distance from us. The tall fae regards us all with his usual haughty air, and I fix my gaze on him to express my distrust.

"Where are the other two?" asks Ripley, breaking our

silent standoff. "You realise this must be an alliance with the five of you, or I won't be able to trust you."

Trust. Ha ha. "Joss and Vee will be here soon," I say.

"I'm very interested to meet her." Ripley smiles. "I didn't get close enough before to shake her hand. To sense what she is."

"Believe me, mate, touching her might not be a good idea." Ewan can't hide his amused smile at Ripley's disconcerted look.

"So she just belongs to you? I get that."

"Vee is unique," puts in Heath. "And you know that."

"Okay, can we talk about what we know, while we wait for your friends," puts in Breanna. "I've seen some of Seth's handiwork. The rune on Taron. That was Seth," she says. Not a question—a sure statement.

"Yeah, I'd love to know who Seth was working with on that day, luring the guy there to put on a show for us."

"I heard about Taron's death," says Ripley. "Whoever helped Seth was human. Easily fooled."

Ewan laughs. "A human beat Seth up? The guy hits like a fucking truck."

"I have no explanation, but thought it was important you didn't blame me." Ripley places fingers on his chest.

I don't know whether to believe him, but it's irrelevant whether I do or not. Taron's death has disappeared off the scale of what's important. Poor guy.

"Taron told us Seth was Chaos," Heath says in a low voice. "He pointed at him and bloody said the words! How dumb are we?"

"Well," pipes up Ripley. "You are quite dumb sometimes. You've missed dozens of opportunities to find me, and then the time you did...well, big fat fail."

I straighten. "Don't push your luck, demon."

"Aww, did I hit a sore spot? I have noticed that as War, you're less of a strategist than the last one, and more on the brawn above brains side."

"The last what?" I shoot back. Someone else taunting us that we weren't the first? Of course we bloody know that, but never realised Ripley did too.

"Ignore him," Heath whispers. "He's trying to get a rise out of you."

I pull out a chair and sit opposite Ripley, and stare straight in his face.

"Yeah. I can hit first and ask questions later."

To show what I mean, I take my dagger out and place it on the table.

"Can we drop the testosterone battle and talk about what we're here for?" Breanna's voice is quieter than before, less sure, and that worries me.

"Fine. Let's talk about the facts we have." Ripley tips his chin at Ewan. "Tell me. You've been at the pointy end of an encounter with Chaos?"

"Yeah."

"And you let him get away."

Ewan mutters something and steps forward, but Heath holds out a hand to stop him and says, "I don't think anybody could stop Seth getting away."

"Where do you think he went? Do you think he's still in Seth's form—the human one, I mean," I ask Ripley.

Ripley looks to Logan. "We spoke about this before. I don't think any of us will find Seth until he decides to show himself. We need to count on Seth having fun with the situation before he finalises his plans."

"We'll find him," says Ewan gruffly. I look around, surprised by his confidence, because mine's gone to hell. "He said he wanted to stop Vee and kill us. I hate to agree with a demon, but yes, before he finishes what he came for, Chaos wants fun."

"Why exactly does he want to do this?" asks Heath. "Why destroy the world by unleashing forces that will devastate the planet and everything living here? That won't leave much for him to rule over."

"He doesn't want to rule. He just wants everything gone." I blink at Ripley's words. "From what Breanna has deduced so far, he's done this before, to other worlds. There are black holes in space—voids—where once there were planets. This goes beyond other realms. Perhaps he wants to wipe the slate clean and start again."

"How the hell could you know that?" snaps Ewan.

"And how do you know his plan is to open the portals?" adds Heath. "Or is that a guess or convenient thing to tell us so we allow you near the area?"

"Because I have read half a story in a book."

"What book?" asks Joss sharply.

"The Collector isn't the only person Syv collects things for," says Ripley with a chuckle. "He likes to collect trinkets, I like books. I've spent the last couple of years tracking down anything that remotely resembles prophecies, and Breanna has helped me translate them."

"And the Collector may have a book we need," puts in Breanna. "One with ancient magic and information about this whole situation. Seth needs to find this book too, so we need to get to it first. We placed one of the runes into Alasdair's foundation's logo. Have you seen a book containing a matching rune at the Collector's?"

I glance at Heath and he nods. "Yes."

"Then it's even more important I read that book. Does he have something to decode it?"

"No, we have a friend helping find something that will."

"Syv, I presume?" Ripley says with a chuckle. "Quite a special girl."

"Then let's hope she finds what we need before Seth finds her," replies Breanna.

I blink. Shit, I hadn't thought about him pursuing her too.

Logan interrupts. "One thing we need to consider while we find this item to translate the text is how to protect the portals, because I'm certain Seth will attack them now. You four—five—cannot do that alone. Myself and Ripley need permission to approach them and have our forces guard without you killing them."

I fight the knee-jerk reaction to tell them to fuck off, because we've spent the last ten bloody years keeping Ripley and others away. So far, we've succeeded, as the portals are warded by someone, or something, that came before us.

In between dealing with the demon issue, we spend time checking they're intact or responding to any indications they're under attack. In recent years, few attempts have been made to open them; the Order have other plans inside the human world, and I suspect they're waiting until their foothold is established before launching an all-out attack on the portal leading to their realm.

With the portals spread across continents, we can't be around all at once, but we're hardwired into them, visions assaulting us with a matching panic if any are touched. So far, no magic exists powerful enough to breach any quickly, giving us time to reach them. Even the ones on other continents. Ripley was close once, the last time we met, and we were close to killing him, but he failed.

Six portals. Six realms. We're aware what lies behind four because the evacuees from the worlds have told us. One, a demon realm linked to the Order, and of course the devastated fae realm. Vampire elders told us one portal leads to a parallel world where vampires rule and are at war with shifters, and the humans are subjugated. The last we know about is an elemental plane, but we've only read about that in Joss's books. I'm not a hundred percent sure exactly what an elemental plane contains, or if anything has crossed through in the past. If they did, they're well-hidden and have zero effect on the human society they now inhabit or avoid.

We have no clue what lies behind the other two.

We're all aware how opening the portal to the demon realm he came from is one of Ripley's goals. How can we trust he won't do that?

This pisses me off the most about the whole thing—having to put my trust into these people. What if this is an elaborate trick and they're in league with Chaos?

Heath answers for me. "If we agree, you can't guard the one you're interested in opening."

"Naturally," says Ripley, and I stare in surprise at his agreement. "I'm happy to deploy people to protect any other portals. I have some military connections, of course."

"Like an army will have a chance against a god!" says Ewan derisively.

He ignores me. "What are the chances of getting Portia onside?" Ripley looks between me and Logan. "You could try between you to persuade her. Together."

My shoulders tense. *Together.*

"Sure, Logan has plenty to explain to Portia," says Heath, and flicks him a tight smile.

"Yeah, Logan, why don't you tell me about the magic you've been buying?" I ask. "What's that all about?"

I wait for a shocked reaction, pissed off when his usually sneering attitude remains. "Isn't that obvious? I was sure

Portia and her court wouldn't help, and I need more powerful fae from elsewhere."

"Who?" asks Heath.

"Those who'll listen. Younger, mostly."

"And you think they can contain the powerful magic Mac gives them?" asks Ewan in a low voice. "What if the magic corrupts them? We could end up with even more shit to deal with."

Logan shrugs. "Ripley can help if the fae troops get out of hand. He's already *dealt* with some just to put the message across."

"Oh great, so no change to the general murder and mayhem then?" I ask Ripley.

He shoots me a tight-lipped smile. "As of now, I'm not interested in petty politics. But a few lives lost is worth saving more, human or fae."

Again, I wait for Logan's protest, but he's nonplussed. Logan indicates he's siding with Ripley to protect the world, but what about afterwards? What happens to the status quo when we fix this crap and everything returns to normal?

Will everything return to normal, because I'm damn sure that's not happening, whatever the outcome with Seth.

"Do we enlist the other races too?" asks Logan. "Vampires? Shifters?"

Ripley wrinkles his nose. "I'm inclined to say not. The more people involved, the more complicated this becomes. They have little to do with us anyway, so they can remain ignorant."

Ewan makes a derisive noise and adds sarcastically, "Yeah, sure. The vamps and shifters won't find out. Not like Seth will miss an opportunity to stir things up."

"I think the time to rally others has gone, Ewan. Didn't

Seth say he's bringing forward his plans? We could have days left. That's why we sort out a strategy today."

"We'll think about it," I growl.

Ripley stands and looks out of the window, fists clenched by his side, and the room descends into a thick, tense silence.

"You realise you don't have the option, Xander," puts in Breanna.

The door behind me clicks open and I sense Joss and Vee enter the room.

"What the fuck?" Logan jumps to his feet and backs away, face transforming into a mask of fear.

I whip my head around, in case Vee's changed her mind and prepared herself to take the room out with powers or weapons.

But she's calm, face curious as her eyes dart from person to person, mouth tightening as her gaze lands on Logan. Joss holds her hand, but he looks more exhausted than when he went to bed last night. Is keeping Vee soothed taking more out of him than we expected?

"What's wrong, Logan?" asks Ripley sharply, turning too. "Do they have weapons; I can't sense any magic."

"Only a huge nuclear one." Logan wraps his arms around himself and shakes his head, closing his eyes before opening them again. They remain filled with fear.

Everybody else's expressions match: mutual confusion.

"Is this Ripley?" asks Vee in a soft voice, pointing at him.

"Okay. Get her out of here." Logan gestures at Vee and looks in desperation at Ripley. "I don't know what the hell she is because I have never seen anything like her before, but if she stays in here, we're fucked."

Ewan moves closer to Vee, so he and Joss flank her. Vee looks up at Joss, who squeezes her hand tighter.

"I want to help." Vee's voice is soft, and as confused as she looks.

"What can you see, Logan?" asks Ripley, tone sharp.

"Energy. Pure energy. Normally I need to concentrate to see a person's true form, but her... she's nothing. I knew I saw darkness, but this... Her human appearance is just a front for others to see."

I swallow hard and ignore my rising panic. If he's lying, Logan's pulling a fucking great acting job.

"She feels human to me," replies Joss in response to Vee's darkening gaze.

I clench my teeth. This could be my excuse to smack the guy at last. "If you want our help, I suggest you calm down."

Breanna studies each of us in turn. "He's right. If I focus hard I can see yours and the others, Xander, but it's constrained and doesn't burn as brightly as Vee's. I can't see it as readily as Logan, but there's a heat and power from her. Perhaps not quite nuclear though." I scowl as she laughs. This isn't fucking funny.

"Was this in your book?" I snap.

"Super Vee?" Breanna rakes a gaze over her again, then points between us with a slender finger. "No. You are. There's talk of your power, which it seems burns out over time. But Vee's is different."

The room spins sideways. This was supposed to be a conversation about saving the world, not a headfuck about who we are.

"What do you mean?" asks Heath and stands too.

"I mean, Vee's energy is reversed. Darker." Breanna chews her lips and studies Vee. "The Four Horsemen are here to keep portals closed, so does this mean she's here to open them?"

Logan straightens. "I fucking knew it! She is here to side with Seth. To destroy you."

"No. That's bullshit. Vee is part of us." Ewan jabs a finger at Breanna. "This demon is only saying these things to keep us worried enough to help you, Ripley."

"Oh, I see and know more than you realise. That's why Ripley has enlisted me. I thought Truth would be a way to defend the portals from Chaos, perhaps even kill him, or maybe she's more."

"Stop this," snaps Ewan. "This is the wrong way to get our help."

Vee speaks up softly and points at the trio wanting to ally with us. "I sense you'd rather I was dead? Funnily enough, I'd like to kill you too."

"Vee!" hisses Joss and pulls her closer.

"What? If they're putting their cards on the table, I am too." She pauses. "I'm telling you all the truth."

"Yes, but what are you, Truth?" asks Logan. "Are you going to bring the apocalypse your lovers were sent to stop?"

Vee stares back, unblinking, and I will her to deny his suggestion.

"I don't know."

As she says the words, her eyes widen and she places her free hand on her chest before gasping.

"Vee?" Ewan reaches out to take hold of her other arm and I push my chair back, as does Heath, ready to prevent or help whatever the fuck is about to happen.

4

Vee

Breanna's words raise the dark anger inside, the one she said I contained, and I ready myself to deny the bullshit she and Logan spew. I am not here to destroy anything apart from inhuman threats to my world. *My* world.

But I don't have a chance to speak. I sense something is wrong, but not in enough time to realise what's happening.

The room draws away from me, growing smaller and smaller, and I grasp onto Joss and Ewan as I lose sight, the world around sucked away. Suddenly, I feel weightless, dragged into a void that fills my head with pressure. Air rushes past my face as the darkness engulfs me and suddenly I'm on the floor, grass beneath my hands and feet. I fight the nausea caused by my insides being jostled around and stare at the damp grass.

No snow.

Warm.

My vision returns and I look to my left. Joss lies on his back staring upwards, thankfully breathing rapidly. Ewan's to my righthand side, unsteady on his feet. "What the fuck just happened?" he asks.

Around me, pine trees, thick and protective, stretch tall above our heads into a bright sky. The hard ground hurts my knees and I stagger upright.

"Where are we?" I ask.

Ewan pats at his clothes and pulls his phone from his pocket.

"More importantly, how are we here?" asks Joss. "Did the fucking demons do this?"

Me. This had to be me. I felt the surge between us, the fact I held on to them both dragged us all to...here. Who knows where?

I say the words even though they sound ridiculous. "I think I teleported."

"Huh?" Joss knocks dirt from his jeans. "That's not one of our powers."

"Thetford Forest." Ewan holds out his phone.

"England? And *here*? How far from the portal?" Joss strides ahead and points. "This way?"

Ewan shakes his head and points south. "That way."

"Portal?" I ask

"Hang on. Did you say teleported?" asks Ewan.

"We've always wanted to be able to teleport to the portals, nice power." Joss snorts, an edge of sarcasm to his voice. "I presume it is a power."

"I don't know." I explain to them what happened, how I felt, and they watch with stony faces.

"You brought us with you somehow?"

"I don't know if I chose this or was pulled here," I protest.

"This is freaking crazy," mutters Ewan. "Come on."

Our weird expedition continues through the forest. Ewan and Joss seem unsteady on their feet, but minutes later I feel no after effects.

"Have you ever teleported?" I ask.

Joss frowns. "How would we do that? We can't."

"No, I mean are there like magical amulets or something?"

Ewan snorts. "Maybe. Ask Syv. She seems to move around the world bloody quickly sometimes."

"Oh sure, next time we meet and have a friendly chat."

We tramp further. Despite the winter cold, I don't feel as cool as I would've before. Joss and Ewan's cheeks turn pink in the freezing wind.

I've no idea what to expect, or what a portal looks like. Joss and Ewan reach a clearing and examine the trees around, counting and touching them.

"Is one here?" I ask.

Ewan rubs his mouth and nods. "The portal will be visible in the centre of this space soon. The wards have been disturbed."

"No guesses who by," mutters Joss.

I'm pulled to a spot close to the centre Ewan points at and I kneel on the ground. Since I stepped into the space, the energy I feel buzzing around my body has grown. Am I being drawn to the portal, or is it drawn to me?

Blue light flickers on the ground, as if fire kindled by sticks, and I watch as it spreads outwards and upwards into a circular pattern. The middle swirls with a rainbow of colours, images distorted behind as I stare into the centre. I tip my head up to see the top as it grows to over seven feet in height and almost as wide.

"Move away, Vee!" Joss grabs my arm and tugs me backwards, pulling me from my wonderment.

"Where does the portal connect to?" I ask.

Joss is about to answer when Ewan's phone sounds a message alert. He scowls down at the screen and thrusts it at Joss. "Fucking Seth! What does this mean?"

I crane my head to look over Joss's shoulder. The words '*The centre cannot hold*' are on his screen and underneath are the words '*guess who*?'

"I fucking knew it!" Ewan jabs a finger at the phone. "Seth was the killer outside our house. And is that more literary shit?"

Joss nods. "The same poem as the line he wrote on the wall when Casey died."

I tense. When he killed Casey. When I denied there was something wrong.

Joss picks up on my thoughts. "How did Seth hide from you, Vee? That's what I don't understand."

"He's a freaking god, Joss. It's not like detecting a demon!" snaps Ewan.

I smile at Ewan, grateful for him reinforcing what I'd hoped.

"Do you think he's here? If we can't detect him, he might be?" I turn 360 degrees, looking around us, but there's no sound, not even cyclists and walkers we passed on our trek here. The portal shimmers in front of us, and I fight the desire to step further forward and touch.

"I'm here," says a familiar voice.

I look upwards, at the guy speaking as if he's arrived for a catch-up with friends.

Seth.

Chaos.

Sitting on a tree branch and looking down on us.

Bizarrely, he still looks the same; I'd convinced myself he was going to disguise himself as somebody different. Seth gives a little wave. I don't miss Ewan step backwards, closer to Joss.

"Hey, Pony Boys. How are you feeling, Ewan?" The guy's grin spreads across his face as we stare at the Cheshire cat several metres high in the tree.

"Fuck you," he mutters in response.

"I wasn't sure if you'd come too." He gestures between us. "Did you teleport because you were next to her? Or touching? Just so I know for next time."

I stare back, fury shaking into my limbs as something deep inside yells at me to attack him.

"Hey, Verity. Keep it calm, right?" asks Seth. "Not like you could reach me."

"Get down from the fucking tree," growls Joss.

He chuckles. "You gonna try and take me on?" His voice lowers. "Ask Ewan what happens if you piss me off."

"You're hiding up a tree," laughs Joss. "Are you scared of Vee?"

"You should be," I call up to him.

"Maybe. Maybe not. I'm hedging my bets."

Ewan gestures at him. "You can't touch us from up there."

Seth sighs and gestures towards the sky. "Don't you hate a sudden storm?"

A black bolt jolts from his fingers, and a dark cloud blots out daylight above us. Seth chuckles as a huge crash of thunder is joined by a lightning bolt hitting centimetres away from Ewan's feet.

"Arsehole," mutters Ewan as he dodges.

"Besides, I prefer the vantage point up here. Should be fun to watch what happens next."

I glare at Seth, weighing up how far my powers go. I

doubt I could climb the smooth, tall trunk to the tree branch he sits in, and if I can teleport I have no clue how to.

Seth links his fingers together and outstretches his hands, cracking his knuckles as he does. "I'd hoped all four of you would arrive, so we could have a little meeting of our own, but sadly no. I guess you can always relay the information back to the other two."

"This is the first meeting I've had with an idiot sitting in a tree!" calls Ewan.

Seth snorts a laugh and waves a dismissive hand, "Seems you morons finally figured out who I am."

"Yeah, someone who pisses me off," replies Ewan.

"I piss you off? You know what pisses me off? Apart from you, of course. All these stupid other so-called gods who come along and pretend my creations are theirs and think they can police my world with their creatures. Demons. Angels. Whatever. I never said they could make these disgusting human things to crawl all over what belongs to me."

I look straight to Joss, whose tired face pales. *Angels and demons.* Is Seth planting doubts again? Or is this true?

"So, anyway," Seth pauses. "Do you mind listening to my story? No? Good." He lowers his voice. "Now, I'm the important one, and that's not just my ego, by the way. Everything around you is a part of me. This world—me. The human fleas crawling on it fucking irritate me. Literally, like an annoying itch. I need them gone."

"Humans have been here years, why come back now?" I ask.

"Oh, this isn't my first time. I created and opened some portals from my other worlds to here a while ago. I thought I'd watch what happened before everybody died." He chuckles. "You know the portals? There's six of them right, pony boys? Well, the stupid other god got in my way and closed them. Or tried to."

Joss's breathing picks up. "What other god?"

Seth throws his hands up in mock despair. "God. The one who thought he could march in here and take over." He points upwards. "You do know about him, surely?"

Ewan shares Joss's shocked look. "Bullshit."

"Fine. Believe what you want. The reason I've been away so long? I had some other business to attend to—you know how it is when people just won't leave your things alone—so now I'm back to fix the mess here."

"He's insane," mutters Ewan. "Don't listen to him."

"And here you are!" He waves his arms as if welcoming us to a party. "The lovely Horsemen and their mysterious Truth. Now *she* was my curveball. I came back expecting to flick you four off the planet and be done, maybe take down an angel or two, if any still exist. Anyway, with *her* around— impossible. God knows I tried too." He chuckles. "God knows? See what I did there?"

"Well, give up and piss off, then!" snaps Ewan. "See this world as the one that got away."

Seth barks a laugh that echoes around the clearing. "Truth is just a roadblock, I'll end her somehow." Ewan tenses. "Now, here's where we have something in common: we both need to know who Vee is and how to use her. I saw the book the Collector has—thanks for taking me to meet him, by the way. Nice guy. This book was presumably created for you all to find. It's definitely connected to me because someone wrote my runes inside, but fuck knows what the rest of it says."

"You're not getting your hands on that book," I say.

He ignores me. "There's something to translate the text. Hidden. Probably some stupid attempt to stop me." He rolls his eyes. "Everything has to be so damn hard. I'm sure that in the book there's the answer to the question we both need to know: what is Truth?"

"She's here to fucking kill you," Ewan calls up to him.

"I need to know if that's true or not. Bring me the book."

"No." My reply is as loud as his laughter before.

"Wrong answer! Try again!" he calls. "Or else things will get really fucking unpleasant, for you and the fleas you protect."

"This conversation is over." Joss turns his back on Seth, then adds in a low voice. "Get away from him."

"Don't fucking walk away from me!" he snarls. "Ewan made that mistake once!"

A low whining noise emanates from behind me, and I snap my head around. A sound like a cacophony of voices comes from the portal, increasing in volume, and my desire to attack Seth suddenly switches to panic.

"What did you do?" asks Joss sharply, looking at the portal.

"This little meet-up is also a test run. I need to see what happens when Vee is close to a portal." He flicks his fingers at where shapes morph in and out of view behind the shimmering colours. "What do you think, Truth? Can you close portals?"

A crackling sound joins the whining, the volume drowning out Ewan's reply to Joss. I focus on watching the portal, a tension flickering down my spine and shooting strength into my limbs, and the familiar tingle caused by magic begins.

"What's behind this one?" I ask Joss.

"We don't know. Nobody ever bothered tampering with this portal, since this is closest to where we're based."

"I don't know, either," pipes up Seth. "Hopefully something interesting."

A black fault line appears down the centre, like an animal's pupil, running from top to bottom and widening. Ewan and Joss move to stand in front of me, and I shove them to one side. We form a line, all transfixed.

"Can you see anything? What is it?" calls Seth. "A dragon? I hope it's a dragon!"

A force rushes through the portal, blurring the surroundings for a moment, and knocks back the guys, but I remain standing, arms outstretched, ready to protect myself and deal with whatever this is.

"Maybe ten dragons!" enthuses Seth.

"I seriously want to rip that guy's fucking head off," Ewan mutters. "What do we do?"

We don't move, and my heart kicks into overdrive as a hulking figure begins to form from behind the spiralling colours. The figure doesn't move for a few seconds, and then a dog appears and springs from the glimmering space.

Not a dog. This is three times the size of the Rottweiler my old neighbour owns, and three times the bulk.

The dog lands on all fours, then looks around with shining orange eyes. The glow surrounding the dog makes him morph in colour between black and red, and it's impossible to see whether the creature has any hair. It's definitely possible to see the unnatural size of its teeth and claws though, especially as the animal rushes Joss with a snarl.

Joss sidesteps in shock, and the dog crashes to the ground. Regaining his footing, the dog turns his head towards Ewan and slobber flies from its mouth, and as it does, hits Ewan on the hand.

"Shit!" Ewan yelps and wipes away the drool. He stares

down at the livid red mark left in a pattern to match where the saliva hit him. "Don't let the bloody thing touch you."

"Uh, yeah, I was planning on avoiding that." Joss calls and backs up. "I left my knife too, because Xander didn't want us all carrying them."

Seth makes a loud tutting sound. "Bloody Xander. Always causes you problems, huh? Vee, can you bring War next time? I'm sure he'd love to see me as much as I want to see him."

Next time?

I wipe a hand down my face and turn back to the portal, focusing my attention away from the dog. The guys will keep the creature off me, I'm sure. We all know one thing: I need to figure out what to do with this portal.

"How do I close it?" I call to the guys.

"No fucking clue. Is anything else coming through?" asks Joss.

"Dragon?" asks Seth and claps his hands together.

"Shut up about fucking dragons!" shouts Ewan as he weaves backwards away from the dog's attacks.

I snap back to studying the portal, pleading with the fate that brought me here to give me the power to solve this. I picture a pack of giant dogs with glowing eyes and poisonous saliva pouring through and charging into the forest—and the world.

Or worse.

That can't happen. I step forward and touch the edge of the glimmering frame, tentative at first. As I do, I see the crowding figures held back by the shimmering barrier. Now I'm closer, I can also see a dark background, mingled with orange, but no buildings visible.

And judging by what just burst through, I don't want to see anything else. My panic joins determination that if there's anything within me that can stop whatever Seth has started, it will.

Snarling and thudding sounds from a fight continue behind me, with Joss and Ewan shouting instructions at each other. Seth remains quiet. I zone away from my surroundings, the way I did the other night standing in the snow, and concentrate on the energy emitting from the portal. My hand glows as I watch, but nothing happens to the portal.

A limb breaks through, blackened, hand held into a claw sweeping from side to side, and panic jerks every muscle inside me. I want this closed. This has to closed. The sound of a dozen dogs growling echoes behind.

Shit.

I move my hands onto the portal, pulling at the energy as if I'm drawing together a rip in fabric. The hand grasping at me slides backwards as the hole begins to disappear and the forest can be seen behind again. I grip on with every ounce of energy—supernatural and physical—praying I can hold this closed long enough.

"Help me!" I call out. "I don't know how you can, but please!" My body trembles as the built-up strength pours through me, dark spots dancing in front of my eyes as the portal grows smaller beneath my hands.

The last thing I hear before I pass out is a snarl followed by a yell and then Joss's voice at my side.

---

*E*WAN

The fucking abomination lands on my chest and I throw it from me. *Well, I expected it to be stronger than that.* It lands with a howl and whimpers, then remains still. Ignoring Seth's running commentary of our battle, as if we're taking part in some kind of fucking football game, I pull myself upright.

Focusing on the dog, I stride over, but am arrested by Vee's cry for help. I turn in time to see Vee thrown backwards from the portal, landing heavily on the ground several feet away. Joss rushes over to her, and all thought of harming the dog leaves as I see her prone body.

"Fuck!" I join Joss and stare down at her pale face, hair tangled in the dirt.

"Aw man!" calls Seth. "That wasn't much fun. Now the dog's hurt too! Is Vee okay?"

I turn on my heel and stomp over so I'm beneath where Seth looks down, blinded by fury. I don't give a shit if he hits me again; he might hurt me but I'm ninety percent confident he won't kill me.

Ninety percent.

"You say you're going to end me? I'm going to fucking end you!" I shout.

"Ooh, you're sounding a bit War-like there, Pestilence." Seth laughs. "Be serious."

"What the fuck is all this about? If you opened a portal, why bring us here to try and stop it?"

"For shits and giggles." He points behind me. "Vee managed to close it though. Don't stress so much! She's fine. Look."

Vee staggers to her feet and pushes hair from her face. The space containing the portal has changed, and only the small blue sparks remain, fizzing on the hard earth.

A figure blurs as the dog charges in my direction. I sidestep, not ready for its attack, but the creature screeches to a halt by the patch on the floor. He sniffs around at the ground and whimpers as the blue energy hits his nose. The blue disappears and the dog begins to dig furiously, a hole a metre across appearing in seconds.

"Kill it!" I hiss at Joss.

The dog stops abruptly, as if hearing my words, and launches itself towards the edge of the clearing, figure blurring into the trees before any of us can move.

"Oopsies. He got away." Seth laughs. "I hope he doesn't hurt anybody."

I ignore him. "Are you okay, Vee?"

She nods and stares down at the hole.

"Do you think this is because you're in the world?" Joss asks. "You were pulled to and closed the portal Seth tried to open. Maybe you do that every time one is threatened."

"I doubt it, or we'd be running in circles forever. I open, she closes, I open, she closes, yada yada," calls Seth.

A thought strikes me. "You're scared of her, aren't you? Look at you, hiding in a fucking tree."

He sneers. "I'm not going to stand in front of an opening portal!"

"Well, you failed. She closed it," snaps Joss.

"This time." He sighs. "Well, now that's over, here's the deal. I have someone looking for something to translate the book too. Syv won't be an issue if she gets in the way because she has less power than you. Bring me the book, Syv stays safe, and the portals stay closed. For now."

"I'm going to end you." The darkness in Vee's voice shocks me as I stare around at her.

"Of course you will," he says in a patronising tone. "But we don't know how you can do that. Or *if* you can."

"We will," I shout.

"Such confidence! I love that!" he calls back. "Would you do whatever it takes, Vee?"

"Yes."

Seth pauses and leans forward. "Even die?"

The forest floor retreats to an eerie silence and I hear my heart hammer in my ears after the fight—and his words. Seth smirks down, leaving his dramatic pause and unanswerable question as the dark void I saw once appears around him and swallows his figure.

Joss rubs his temples as we stand, the three of us dishevelled and in shock. I reach out to Vee, who stares at the ground, face hard, and she allows me to fold her in my arms. Joss approaches too and we stand and hold her, sharing the same thought.

Vee. Die?

Is Seth causing chaos with his words, as he did with breaching the portal's defences, or does he know something we don't?

5

Joss

Man, today is a headfuck.

Literally, because teleporting into the centre of a popular tourist spot made my brain feel as if it's been slammed back and forth against my skull.

So a brisk walk in the November cold, freezing my ears and balls off isn't helpful. We set off towards the National Park's visitor centre, fortunate we were dressed for cold weather and a quick getaway thanks to our rudely-cut-short meeting with Ripley and co.

I've barely had time to think about this since, the last hour felt like a lifetime, a world away from unnatural alliances. Seth's words about angels and demons ring in my ears, and however hard I try to tell myself he spun us a story, the broken memories inside my head tell me otherwise.

Now, more than ever, I believe I've come from Hell. But where is that? One of the other portals?

We don't mention Seth. His change in personality shouldn't have been a shock, but his inane and childish behaviour was.

"What do you think happened to the dog?" asks Vee.

I shake myself out of my thoughts. Vee links her arms through both of ours, side by side; I expected her to be damaged or exhausted after she closed the portal, but Vee's her bright self. Her new self. Yes, she's the same Vee, but I sense a difference in her, a new heat from her skin and a power within stronger than before. What did Logan mean about her being pure magic? That's nonsensical. She's a living, breathing girl. I couldn't be in love with someone who had no heart.

My physical need for Vee has multiplied to an uncomfortable, obsessive level. Her touch has always sparked desire that shot through my veins and enthralled me, and now that beauty and desirability drives me to distraction when all I'm doing is breathing the same air. Is this the same for the others? Xander went straight to her last night, and Ewan kept her close too.

I don't doubt whatever power she now contains engulfs us all.

If Vee drops one hint that she wants me, I'm there and not holding back. This worries me, because all along I've fought and controlled the lust in an attempt to stay loving and attentive. The deeper, primal Joss wants her hard and fast, under my control for once.

I swallow and look upwards, focusing on the sky and not images of me smacking Vee's bare ass.

Fuck, Joss.

"Do you think we should? I'm not sure if things would

get out of control. Someone might get hurt." Vee nudges me in the side. *Shit.* Is she a mind reader now too?

"What?" I ask hastily.

"The dog," says Ewan gruffly. "Vee wonders if we should catch it."

"That isn't a bloody dog!" I half-laugh. "Ten quid says that's a new brand of demon we've not met before."

Vee bites her lip. "I worry about what it might do to people. It's our fault the dog is here."

I snort. "Um. Seth's fault."

"Have you seen my hand?" Ewan stretches out his arm and a red welt covers the back. "If that's from the demon's saliva, imagine what his teeth and claws could do."

Vee takes his hand and looks down at it. "Ewan, you didn't say he hurt you!"

"It doesn't hurt." He pulls his fingers away and Vee grabs them again.

With a small smile, she lowers her mouth to the sore and places her lips on it while Ewan looks on in consternation.

I laugh. "You know Vee can always kiss things better."

Ewan looks at his hand as she lets go, and the frown deepens. He swipes a finger across his skin. "Literally."

"What?"

His hand is no longer red. Wow. I know we heal quickly, but not from a kiss or touch. Vee chews on her bottom lip. "I wanted to check it wasn't a coincidence."

"What do you mean?" I ask.

"Last night, I touched Ewan's bruises and they disappeared. Now this injury has too." Her eyes glint as she looks up at us. "Do you think this means I might be able to go further?"

"And resurrect?" I ask.

She nods vigorously and hugs us, one and then the

other. "Yes. This must mean I have a healing power—maybe I can develop this to more?"

As we wrap our arms around her, I exchange a hopeful look with Ewan. No more death? No more visions... I blink them away as they encroach, the way they do almost hourly.

But we can't be confident her powers would stretch that far.

My thoughts turn to our brief communication with a confused Xander and Heath. "What did Xander say in his text?" I ask Ewan.

"They're driving back from Scotland now, but that's hours. He's trying to contact Syv to see if she's in the area. I know she's scouring the bigger museums currently. She might be in London."

"So a couple of hours away if she is and wants to help?" asks Vee.

After Seth's words about her, I'm worried about Syv and bloody hope Xander can find her.

"Did you tell Xander what happened?" asks Vee.

"No. Not much. Just that we saw Seth and what happened with the portal." Ewan avoids my eyes. *Not the story of God and angels.*

"Probably a good idea to wait until he and Heath are back and we're all home." Vee digs her hands in her pockets. "We can wait at the visitors centre and decide what to do."

The number of people milling around increases the closer we get to the Park's centre at the edge of the forest. Cars fill the car park, some with bike racks where suitably dressed people in helmets are pulling the bikes down to the ground, and a teacher counts a busload of kids climbing from inside. The cold pinches my cheeks, and I'm eager to get inside the building and wait for Syv.

My phone sounds and I look down at the message. "It's

Syv. She wants us to meet her at a track a mile away. She'll be an hour."

"For fuck's sake!" exclaims Ewan. "Why?"

"Who knows? Maybe she's avoiding public appearances." Ewan crosses his arms and pouts in a way that would give Elyssia a run for her money. "Or y'know, we can wait around for a bus or taxi, Ewan. Just feel fortunate she's doing this for us."

This isn't the first time I've longed for a teleportation charm or spell. Seriously, being able to move from portal to portal easily makes so much bloody sense, but not to whoever put us here. *Yeah, thanks for that.*

"I don't know her well, but I'd hazard a guess Syv may be pissed off if she drove here and didn't find us."

I blow air into my cheeks. Vee's right. Of course. We need Syv on side, and here's the perfect opportunity for a chat.

I stride away, still holding Vee's hand, and Ewan's heavy footsteps soon follow. The forest becomes denser for a few hundred metres before thinning out towards a dirt track used as a service access point. A large, padlocked metal box is beneath a tree, with the park property stamp on the side. Tools for maintenance?

A beaten-up Jeep is parked beside it at the end of the rough track. Syv sits on the bonnet, arms hugging her knees as she watches us approach. Her long auburn hair is loose across her shoulders for once, giving her angular features a softer look. She's swapped leather for denim, but the jeans hug her legs just as tightly and end in the same heavy motorcycle boots. I guess she's always wary who she'll need to kick. She wears a padded green jacket and fingerless gloves, and in her hand twirls one of the curved daggers she favours.

I arch a brow and indicate the knife. "That's a friendly welcome."

"Oh." She looks at the weapon as if she forgot she's holding it. "Habit. Always playing with my toys." She shoves the dagger back inside her boot. "You took your bloody time."

"Busy day," replies Ewan before crossing to the car. "I don't want to hang around any longer than you do."

Syv twists her head around to watch Ewan as he reaches for the car door handle. "I wouldn't do that if I was—"

She's interrupted by a snarl and a loud thump as something throws itself against the rear passenger window.

Ewan steps back. "What the fuck?"

The window mists as a canine face presses against it, drool spreading across the window from the creature's slavering mouth.

"Is that...?" asks Vee, keeping her distance.

"I found him. Well, he found me." She cranes her head, unperturbed by the vicious snarling and barking. "Odd really, I didn't know anything like him existed in this world."

"What is it?" Vee asks.

"A demon. Not sure what. Canine." She giggles and says 'woof' at Ewan, whose face hardens. "I don't bloody know. He seemed friendly enough to me, so I thought I'd pick him up. I doubt the locals want to meet him."

"Friendly?" I choke. "He attacked us before, when he came through the portal."

Syv hops down from the car, snarky look evaporating. "What portal?"

"Seth opened one. Chaos. Has anybody mentioned Seth's a god intent on destroying the world? No?" Ewan's eyes harden. "Such as Breanna, who you're also working for?"

Syv's mouth falls open. "Whoa. What the...that's fucked up. I should chat to Col, see what he knows." She blinks. "Hang on, is there a fucking portal open? Where?"

"No. We closed it, but not before he ran out." Ewan jabs a finger at the still-snarling dog.

"Poor thing!" exclaims Syv.

"Excuse me?"

"He's trapped here, alone. I bet you scared the crap out of him."

"Oh yeah, look, he's terrified." Ewan points.

Syv tuts and shakes her head. "You obviously know nothing about dogs."

"That monster is not a fucking dog!" He gives a harsh laugh. "What are you going to do? Take it to the RSPCA?"

"No, I'll take him home. I bet he'd make a great guard dog."

"Are you serious?"

"I can't just leave Spot out here. He could attack humans." She smiles around at the dog. "Besides, he likes me."

"Spot?" Ewan and I ask in unison.

"Yes. So do you want a ride or what? I'm a busy girl."

"How are we supposed to get in your car if some creature from another realm, who clearly wants to kill, is in there?" Ewan points again.

Syv sighs and opens the car door.

"Fuuuuck." Ewan and I step back while Vee nervously joins us.

The dog jumps out and I stare as Syv scolds the animal for barking. It crouches at her feet, hackles up. "I'll put him in the back. You'll be fine."

She crosses to the car boot and lifts the door. The Jeep

has a bar between the boot space and the back seats. "Coming or not?" asks Syv as she slams the door closed.

I eye the open passenger door, debating what to do. Vee mutters something about how she wants to get home and climbs in. Alarmed the dog might attack, I join her.

The car smells of stinking dog breath, and when I close the window I can't see anything through the mist on the pane. Ewan joins Syv in the front and we lapse into silence, besides the heavy panting and low growl from the creature separated from us by metal.

Metal I'd bet he could chew through if he wanted.

6

Vee

Syv's battered Jeep is parked outside the house, an uncomfortable reminder nobody else here has a car. Ewan lost his shit about his bike stuck in Scotland and Joss wasn't amused that this was on Ewan's priority list. Joss is right, Ewan's bike is the least of our current problems.

Xander and Heath are on their way back but will be hours yet. I watch through the lounge window as Syv stands with Spot, now leashed by rope. Ewan and her continue an argument that started in the car about what to do with him. I tiptoe to watch as Syv stomps away with her new pet in tow.

Joss wanders in with an amused smile.

"Aren't you worried? The dog attacked you," I ask.

"A little. Ewan's telling her to put him in the old barn."

"Good thing nobody's cars are parked in there." Xander in particular likes to keep his Aston under cover, and the barn makes a makeshift garage. I doubt he'd like it chewed or clawed up by a demonic dog.

"Yeah." Joss cups my cheek. "How are you feeling after our surprise journey and encounter?"

I smile at Joss's attempts to make light of everything again. "We have a lot to chat to Heath and Xander about when they get home."

"That'll take another three hours, apparently."

The front door slams and the windows shake before Syv appears in the lounge. She strips off her green jacket and dumps it on the sofa. Beneath, she wears a black singlet with a large blue stone on a necklace, hanging between her full breasts. She drags her fingers through her hair, pulling it out of her face, and a tattoo across her wrist shows itself. A black symbol, intricate and hard to make out at a distance.

"I locked Spot in the barn. Now I need a drink." She strides past us into the kitchen, and cupboard doors bang open and closed until the chink of glass can be heard. She reappears in the doorway with a bottle and four glasses. "Here. Something for the shock?"

"It's 4 p.m., Syv," says Joss.

"Who gives a fuck?" She thrusts a glass at him and sloshes in whiskey. "Vee?"

"Uh." My protest is silenced as she pours and passes me a drink too.

"Yeah." Ewan strides into the kitchen behind her and holds out a hand. "I need one."

Drinks distributed, Syv pulls herself onto the kitchen counter and sits, sipping as she watches the three of us.

"Get me up to speed then. I've been hunting for this artefact you're all keen to find. Xander told me things are more complicated now but didn't elaborate." She slurps. "Man, he was in a bad mood. What's with this Chaos thing?"

Joss makes a derisive sound. "'Chaos thing'. You don't know how bad this is."

"Enlighten me." Syv pours herself another drink.

We spend the next half hour filling Syv in with all the details about what's happening, and the events of the last twenty-four hours. Her face switches between surprise and shock before she pulls her neutral expression back on.

I don't miss that she drinks more quickly as the story continues, her pink cheeks and troubled look growing as her name is mentioned.

"I guess I'd better find this artefact you need and quickly," she says eventually. "Thanks for sending a god after me."

"We didn't send him. If Seth has someone following you, I think he's confident you'll find the object more easily than anyone else. Do you think you can?"

Syv smiles proudly, then drains her glass. "If I walk into a museum or antique store, every magic item attracts me. Do you know how many types are out there? Fae. Druidic. Elemental. Demonic. A shitload. I think I know what I'm looking for now, but it's still tricky."

"Maybe your new pet can help you," suggests Ewan with snark. "He could sniff something out."

"Ah, who knows. I bet he has some special skills," she replies.

"Yeah, like the ability to rip people to shreds in seconds."

"Don't worry your pretty face, Ewan. I'll protect you."

He scowls.

"One thing's for sure, I'm hanging 'round you guys for protection." She hops down and wanders back into the lounge, calling, "Want to see my new weapons?"

I watch her go. All females I've met since my arrival in this life haven't been friendly. Syv is non-committal towards me, but that beats Portia's rudeness and Breanna's quiet suspicion.

Syv walks back in carrying two thin-bladed daggers, gripping them by the ornately carved handles. The blades catch the kitchen light and dazzle, and I'm pleased they're bloodstain-free.

Syv twirls one in her hands before setting it on the table. "My weapons are prettier than yours, boys. Still using bowie knives?" Syv taps her palm across her open mouth, faking a yawn. She winks at me and I smile at her teasing. "Here, what do you think of mine?"

I take the proffered dagger and weigh it in my hand. It's lighter, and she's correct, it's prettier, the blade thinner and sharper than the ones the guys give me.

What do I say? I've no clue how to discuss the merits of instruments of death. "Nice."

She cups a hand around her mouth so the guys can't hear her next word to me. "Fae."

"Oh. Is that a good idea?" Is this what Portia was talking about when she accused Syv of stealing something important?

"Nah. Ten a penny. You can find them in antique shops all over. Col wants them all; he's not happy about fae items strewn across the world. That's most of what I collect for him."

Ewan takes the dagger and places it on the table. "As interesting as your life is, we've more important things to deal with than your shady business dealings and unimpressive weapons."

Syv cocks a brow. "Gonna show me your weapon then, Ewan? Is *that* impressive?"

I laugh as Joss groans at her descent into childish laughter. Ewan makes an exasperated noise and picks up his glass. "Joss. I want to research Chaos, demonic dogs, and how to shut up cheeky mercenaries."

Syv smirks and flicks him on the nose. "You know I'll always help you. I owe you. Well, Xander, anyway."

My ears prick up. I've heard a few references to Xander and Syv, and the possibility they may've been intimate had niggled, but this sounds like something different.

Ewan looks to me. "Are you okay, Vee? We can stay with you and talk about what happened?"

I shake my head. "I'd rather wait until Xander and Heath get home. I'm kind of okay."

"Kind of?"

I scrunch my face up. "Kind of. Don't ask me questions." Joss and Ewan exchange troubled glances and I reach out to touch Joss's arm, who's closer. "Like Syv, I need a drink."

Is Joss going to push this? He chews on his lip, then nods. "Okay, keep Syv company," says Joss.

Syv watches them go and shakes her head. "They mean stay with me and make sure I don't steal anything."

I nod, because I've no idea what to say. She wouldn't steal from the Horsemen. Would she?

I'm still processing what happened to me and why. The meeting where I was told I'm a supernatural nuclear bomb. The teleporting. Seth. Closing a portal. It's all too much for my brain to deal with at once.

The teleportation—or whatever it was—didn't hurt or scare me, but I knew the portal was close by before the guys told me. Am I linked to the portals somehow? Or Seth? If I'd been close enough, I wouldn't have been able to stop myself attacking him. I barely have any recollection of closing the portal or how I did; it was an instinctive response as if I was standing back and watching myself.

No, my biggest fear is how suddenly everything happened and how I had no control.

Syv slaps both palms on the table and squints at the now-empty bottle. "I hope they have more."

"Their house is always stocked with alcohol." I point at the top cupboard.

When Syv places shot glasses and a half bottle of tequila in front of me, I weigh up what to do. Despite the amount I've drank, I don't feel as intoxicated as I may've been before. Looks like Syv can hold her liquor well too.

Syv spots my hesitation as she hovers the bottle above a small glass. "I don't often hang out with people. I want to have some fun."

"What about Abel?" I ask.

She purses her lips as she swaps to pouring into the second glass. "We don't spend much time together. We're a long-distance friends with benefits. He's in the States a lot."

I suck my lips together, unsure if I should say the next words. My mind flashes back to the last time I saw her other acquaintance, Taron.

Y'know. The time I killed him.

She grimaces as she takes a shot. "I don't get attached. It gets messy, and I'm too busy."

"I'm sorry about what happened to Taron, though. I know he was your friend."

"Occupational hazard—that's the cliché term, right?"

"I guess..." I stare down at the shot glass filled with clear liquid.

"You're going to ask me why I do all this, aren't you?" She taps her fingers on the table. "The usual. Money. No education past high school, no skills apart from bartending or waitressing." She grimaces. "Laying out punters who grope my arse doesn't offer job security. Using my unique skills? Profitable, and maybe one day I'll find out more about myself. A journey of self-discovery!" She ends her little speech by flourishing her hands in the air.

"Because you're half-demon?" Man, I'm bold after a few drinks. This girl has sharp knives and a temper to match her hair, I'll bet.

"And half kickass awesomeness." She chuckles, but with every word, I pick up something else. The alcohol pulls away some barriers she may not realise are coming down. She's lost and unsure. Desperate for answers.

I know the feeling.

"I'm sure you are. How long have you known the Horsemen?"

She nods at my glass. "Drink."

I obey, and the fiery liquid burns my throat. I thought whiskey was bad, but this? Ugh.

"You want to know what about Xander and if we have a past, don't you? I've seen the look on your face when I mention him."

"Yes." I place a hand over my mouth. *Go me and my truth-telling.*

She laughs. "Don't worry, I haven't screwed him if that's what worries you. That arrogant ass isn't my type, and the Horsemen were never fans of my activities. Anyway, I was in a difficult situation once. Xander was there and helped me out of it. We called a truce, and I agreed to help him when needed." She punctuates her staccato story with a long drink. "So yeah. That."

"Must've been bad if you still owe him."

Her lips thin. "Years ago. Forgotten about. I lived."

She clamps up. I could've guessed she's somebody who doesn't welcome questions.

"How about you, Vee? I hear stories about you, and I'm

curious. I know the guys have no clue where they came from, and you don't either, but who's the real Vee? You know, the person behind Truth."

I focus on drinking, afraid because I ask myself that question too much. "The Fifth, apparently."

"With four hot guys smitten by you. I'm not into the whole protective male thing, but it's gotta boost a girl's ego."

I can't stop the grin on my less-than-sober face. "It does. Sometimes more than others, but it's partly why I'm here to unite us against..." The dark reality sneaks into our relaxing afternoon.

"Chaos?" Syv interrupts. "Tell me about him. Man, that sneaky bastard had me fooled. All of us."

"Perks of being a god, I guess."

Syv spins the dagger around on the table as she listens, face impassive. "I think you're doing the right thing, working with Ripley. He's correct—if we don't ally, then we all end up dead."

"I don't think we have a choice. But it doesn't mean anybody will trust him."

"I don't think that's necessary; you can all keep separate. Keep your secrets."

I drink. "The guys are worried Ripley will open a portal to let his leader through."

"That'd be dumb. If Seth wants to open them all, then Ripley opening one would give him a head start. Besides, if you're uh...attracted to portals when Seth tampers with them, Ripley won't have much chance." She taps her dagger against her chin. "Maybe that's why the Order wanted to kill you before the Horsemen found you. They knew you'd stop the portals opening and end their plans."

Hearing the opinion of someone outside of our group, apart from Seth's lies, is weird but welcome. How much does Syv know about how the guys operate? I get a sense she attempts neutrality with every client, or potential client, but that must be tricky and involve double-crossing at some point.

She catches my expression. "But, I hear you're too strong for anybody to touch you now. You must be, if you're going to take down a god."

I gulp the mouthful of tequila and stare back, eyes watering. "Excuse me?"

"Personally, I don't think you're here to help Seth, so it must be your role to take him down."

Her stated opinion shouldn't be a surprise, it's what's been discussed, but I also don't want this to be the truth.

"But we'll know for sure once we've decoded this book and found out what the prophecy is."

This time I almost choke. "Prophecy?"

Syv waves a dismissive hand. "Well, there's always a prophecy, isn't there?"

"Can we talk about something else, please?" I ask and pour the shots this time. "Tell me a story, I bet you have plenty."

Syv leans back in her chair and pulls hair from her face. "Oh yeah, lots of stories. Want to hear the one about my weekend with a vampire rock star?"

I blink rapidly. "There's a vampire rock star? Who?"

Her mouth tips into a sly smile. "That's my secret. You want to hear?"

I scratch my nose. "Does it have a happy ending? I don't want to hear about anybody dying."

Syv leans forward, her blue stone pendant touching the table as she does, and whispers. "A very happy beginning, middle, and ending."

Omigod, is she about to share her sexual conquests with me?

At my expression, Syv barks a laugh. "Nah, he wanted me to find him something magical, of course. We just had some fun in the process."

Syv relays her story with enthusiastic hand gestures and whispers, stopping herself mentioning his band or name a couple of times. A happy glow spreads through, as I feel strangely relaxed by a chat with a friend. Well, the closest to a female friend I've found so far.

Fuzziness in the room joins the warm glow inside. I don't think I've ever drunk this much and managed to stay upright. Old Vee would be slumped asleep on the table - or vomiting - by now.

Halfway through Syv's story, the front door bangs open and closed, and I hear voices in the lounge. I'm torn between politely letting Syv finish her tale and rushing through to see Heath and Xander. I strain to hear their conversation as they talk to Ewan and Joss.

"So, which one?" asks Syv.

Nobody appears, and the guys' conversation continues, so I look away from the doorway back to Syv, who seems oblivious to the fact I've missed the last part of her story. I have no idea what she's asking me, but I'd seem rude if she knew I wasn't listening.

I attempt an answer. "Uh. Who? Um... I don't know."

"One of them must be." Syv's amused smile reaches her flushed cheeks. "Heath? Wasn't he the guy you wanted before you met the others? Did you and him get it on before?" I look back, blankly. "Ooh...Ewan! There's a tension ready to be unleashed there. Man, I bet he's good."

My cheeks flare as I join the dots. Is Syv asking me what I think she is? Which guy's the best between the sheets? Or against the wall? Or wherever. "Uh," I repeat, dumbstruck.

"No? Hmm. Joss? I guess with the empath thing he'd be

very in tune with what works for you." I open my mouth to tell Syv to keep her voice down, but she interrupts. "C'mon, who's the best?"

"Sounds like I walked in on an interesting conversation." Xander leans against the kitchen door frame, arms crossed. "What about me?"

Syv sinks back in her chair with a wide smile. "Hey, Xan."

Omigod how long has he been there?

His calculating gaze travels from the now almost empty bottle of tequila beside the empty whisky bottle and glasses, then to Syv, finally landing on me. My flushed cheeks and blinking attempt to focus on him confirms to Xander what's obvious here.

"Well?" he asks me. "I'm interested to hear your answer."

I silently curse Syv. "How was the drive from Scotland?"

Xander's gaze remains trained on mine, just long enough for me to squirm and convince me he's about to continue the line of questioning.

"Long. Now I need a debrief," he replies.

Syv giggles like a thirteen-year-old and Xander shoots her a look. "About what happened with Seth and why there's a bloody hellhound in my shed."

"That's unfair, Xander. He might not be, we don't know Spot came from Hell. He could just be a normal demon," retorts Syv.

Xander snorts. "Of course. That makes it so much better. I've never come across anything like that before, so get rid of it before I do."

Syv straightens and glowers at him. "Touch him, and I'll hit you. Hard."

"Sure you will."

"Don't piss her off, Xander," I put in. "If she wants to keep him, that's her choice."

Xander shakes his head. "You're insane. Both of you." He gestures at the table. "And drunk."

"Want a drink?" asks Syv and lifts the bottle.

"Maybe later. Vee, if you're sober enough, can you come through to the lounge and talk?"

Syv yawns loudly. "I'll leave you all to your chat. Can I borrow someone's bed? I'll take a nap, then leave later."

Xander closes his eyes and inhales. "Fine."

Syv wanders by Xander, before pausing in the doorway. "Thanks for the fun afternoon, Vee."

I stand too and stumble slightly, steadying myself on a chair. Xander's mouth curls. "Seriously, Vee?"

"What?"

"Getting wasted with Syv. Not helpful."

"I'm fine." I swallow down a hiccup and walk towards him. "I can talk, but I'm sure Ewan and Joss have the full story too."

Before I can walk through the door, Xander wraps his hand around my arm. As with all the guys right now, standing close evokes images of sex and a desire to press my body and mouth against his.

I moisten my lips as I look back into his green eyes. I could wind my arms around his neck, pull him closer, tug that lip into my mouth and bite. Not too hard, just enough. Then he could kiss me until my toes curl and —

"Vee."

I blink at his stern tone. "Sorry. Distracted."

A muscle ticks in his jaw. "That's the problem right now. Stay focused."

"Yes, sir." I snicker again, and Xander huffs, the breath sweeping my face.

Peeling his fingers from my arm, I pass, shoulder brushing his chest. He lowers his voice. "I'd love to know the answer to Syv's question."

Is he joking around or annoyed? As usual with Xander, I can't tell.

Unable to resist, I answer. "Joss."

Xander doesn't reply, but surprise flickers across his face before he blinks it away. "Right."

"Joss is the best driver. Why, what did you think Syv was asking?" I ask with mock innocence.

As I walk away, I bite the side of my hand to stop myself laughing. This is awesome. New Vee can even tell half-truths.

But I've no idea what the answer would be to Syv's real question.

7

VEE

Back to serious, or an attempt to be. Is this my remaining human side trying to blot out the world rather than let the fear take over? I sit on the sofa between Heath and Ewan, head lolling onto Heath's shoulder. Heath fussed around me, repeatedly asking Joss to confirm I'm okay. Thank god Ewan and Joss can tell the bones of the story.

While I was talking with Syv, Joss and Ewan gave the other two a rundown on what happened. Heath and Xander quiz me over how I closed the portal. I can't fully explain how due to the fact I'm drunk and because I barely remember anything but the overriding need to do it. In Xander's eyes I see what's inside me—frustration that Seth has done something we again don't fully understand. We still don't know what I'm capable of—evidently not zapping smirking gods out of trees.

I rest my head on Heath's shoulder and he curls an arm around me. "Are you okay after what happened?"

"Teleporting, or seeing Seth?" I mumble.

"Both," replies Xander. "I'm annoyed we weren't all there."

"I don't think it's time to confront Seth yet, is it? Look at what he is." Despite the sense in Joss's words, I can tell Xander isn't amused.

"But how did it happen? That's what I don't understand." asks Heath.

I shift to rest my head against his chest, burrowing my cheek into his soft warmth and soothing myself with his scent. Please let the room stop spinning.

"Vee?"

"I don't know. I suppose Seth did it somehow."

"How did you feel when you saw Seth?" asks Heath.

I push hair from my face. "Pissed off. I wanted to hurt him before he hurt one of us."

"Do you think you could? Did you feel stronger?" Xander sits forward. "Anything helps us here."

"I don't know, Xander. I felt a strong connection to the portal energy, but my response to him was emotional. Like when you're at full War power. If he'd been close I wouldn't have thought first, I would've just smashed the bastard."

I glare at Joss as he laughs. "Sorry!" He holds his hand up. "The image in my head is a good one."

"This is a double-edged sword," replies Xander. "Vee can somehow teleport to threatened portals—presumably—but that makes it bloody hard to know when this might happen."

"Maybe I'll learn to control the feelings?" I suggest.

Xander scrunches his nose up. Obviously, he doesn't agree.

He's right. What if I suddenly disappear in the middle of the night? If Seth now knows I'm connected, then he can use that to his advantage. The silence tells me I'm not the only one considering this could happen.

"Vee healing Ewan is good," puts in Heath. "I know we don't talk about the topic because you think it'll freak me out, but I'm confident if we die when we confront Seth, Vee can help."

Heath's statement jerks me alert and I cling to his arm. He folds a hand over mine and squeezes. If *he* dies.

"I don't think we look for Seth until we have all the information we can find. There must be a way to take him down; it's obvious us and Vee are the connection or he wouldn't have spent weeks playing with us."

"What do we make of his story?" asks Heath in a quiet voice. "Was he telling the truth or messing with us?"

"We know he's the god of Chaos, so some of it makes sense," I say.

"I think Heath means the part about god, angels and demons, and what we might be," says Joss quietly.

Is this it? Is this the moment their fears are finally shared, and Joss's experiences listened to?

"It means Seth lived with us long enough to pick up on what we worry about by listening in to conversations." Xander drinks the beer he'd fetched himself. "Even I heard you talking to Vee about your biblical stuff. I wish you wouldn't obsess about that shit."

"Why are you in constant denial about this?" asks Joss. "You've had visions too."

"Dreams." He swigs again. "Not visions."

But I saw something in Xander when we were in the hotel room; when our bodies and minds connected I saw and felt screaming and pain. Screaming and pain Joss has experienced and described to me.

"I know but—"

"Change the subject," snaps Xander. "Falling for Seth's mind games isn't helpful right now. God and his band of merry angels is a fabrication. Look at Ripley—him and the demons aren't from Hell, but a different realm. Ripley told us that once. Chaos is the god who created all this."

I wait for Joss to push the topic, hoping he doesn't because I'm too drunk and exhausted for theological arguments.

"Fine. Did you finish your meeting with Ripley?" asks Joss eventually.

"Cut short," replies Xander.

"What did you decide about Portia?" Ewan asks.

"Another double-edged sword." Heath pushes hair from his face. "If we don't tell her, she'll lose her shit when she finds out. If we do, Logan and she will likely be distracted by an internal fae war."

Xander nods. "Then we tell her, but not who's involved."

"She won't go near demons."

"Neither would we two days ago. Portia always demands we tell her everything, so maybe we should. Whether she wants to believe us or not is up to her."

"Logan seems to think he can take on the role of diplomat himself," puts in Heath.

Xander leans back in his chair. "Uh huh. I doubt his motives. I doubt all their motives."

Heath sighs. "I know, but today we saw what Seth is capable of. At least before the meeting ended, we agreed to share defending the portals' wards from breaking. That should hopefully keep Vee in one place, if Seth touching the portal is what caused her to teleport."

Joss laughs, and I frown at him. "Sorry, it just sounds so weird."

"Here we fucking go again," says Heath in a harsh tone. "Back on the merry-go-round."

"No." Xander leans forward hands on knees. "We're not. We've learned Seth still wants to play with us. We know what his aim is, and we know Vee is—" He pauses and glances at me.

"On your side? Not his?" I suggest.

Xander casts his eyes down. "Yeah. Sorry, Vee."

I shrug. "S'okay. Took you long enough." But it's not. The fact even the smallest doubt remains, hurts.

"You spoke to Syv—has she found what we need yet, Vee?"

"Not yet. She's closer though."

"We definitely need to help her out now," says Joss. "Seth threatened her."

"Where *is* Syv?" asks Joss.

"In your bed, comatose, probably," Xander replies. "I'm surprised Vee isn't."

"Surprised Vee isn't in my bed, or isn't comatose?" Joss smirks.

Everybody ignores him and he sighs.

"Yeah, you stink of alcohol, Vee," says Heath. "How much did you have?"

I attempt a focused smile. "I'm fine. Tired. The teleporting thing freaked me out. Besides, it was nice to chat to a female for a change."

Xander laughs. "Oh yeah, girl talk."

"No, actually," I protest. "She was telling me stories about her life. It was good to know mine isn't the weirdest."

"Just be careful," says Ewan. "She's not one hundred percent trustworthy."

"I think she's more trustworthy than Ripley and his colleagues," I reply.

"Yeah, what about Breanna?" he asks. "Do you think she can help? How closely linked is she to Ripley? In ten years, we've never come across her before."

Joss taps the table. "If she has skills at translating texts, I think we should ask her to help next time we see her. I can show her the book we have too. I've never quite deciphered everything."

"Which one?" asks Xander. "You have a crapload of books."

"The one with the Four Horsemen in," Joss replies.

I can't resist a drunk giggle. "The one with the pornographic pictures."

Xander snaps his head around. "What?"

"Vee means that detailed illustration of the four of us with her," says Joss and we share an amused look.

Xander runs his tongue along his teeth. "You showed her *that*?"

"Don't worry, Xander, I won't be asking for a demonstration," I say.

Our eyes meet, but he says nothing.

I flick a look between Ewan and Heath too, attempting to gauge their reaction. I already know Joss's thoughts. Heath watches me curiously. Is he waiting for my opinion?

Ewan stands. "I need some space. I hope Syv didn't crash in my bed."

"Nice subject change, dude," says Joss.

He huffs. "Like Vee said, not going to happen. I won't be joining in if you do."

I stare at my hands, annoyed with myself for my joke, because Ewan's tone isn't amused.

"Whatever, we'll show the book, and anything else we

think might help," says Joss. "We have to do everything we can to solve this."

"We have to figure out how to stop it. Vee suddenly disappearing isn't good."

"You're telling me!" I say with a laugh.

"Next time you feel the same sensations, tell us. Nobody leave Vee alone. Ever." Xander stands. "Okay?"

"Even the bathroom?" I hiccup again. "Seriously? Oh! What if it happens when I'm naked or we're..." I trail off. "Yeah. This is bad."

Despite the alcohol taking the edge off my concerns, I'm worried. Is this random and connected to the portals, or some control Seth has over me? The idea it's the latter churns my stomach.

8

XANDER

Vee stands at the kitchen sink and the glass she holds beneath the tap overflows as she stares out the darkened window. I switch off the tap and take her glass, and Vee blinks at me as she returns to the here and now.

"Are you okay?" I ask her.

She wipes the water that spilled on her hand onto her shirt. "I think so. Are you?"

"No." Because why lie to her?

"I thought about what we said. I don't understand what shifted inside me, but I do know he won't succeed now."

He. Chaos. Fucking Seth. I rub my temples, wishing I shared her confidence.

"I need to tell you something." Vee touches my hand and I drop my fingers in surprise. "I saw something else in that vision, Xander," she whispers. "I saw him. You all."

"Bad?"

Vee looks away and closes her eyes. I think she's retreated from me again, until she opens them and looks straight into mine. Ewan told me what happened in the room, how he saw nothing, but she reacted as if something attacked her, and I've waited for her to tell me.

There's a strange shift in how I feel about Vee. The connection feels stronger, as if the hold over me grew, and I sense myself within her more than I did before. I'm enmeshed tightly, and I don't think I can unpick that now. Ever.

Vee relents and describes what happened. She refuses to tell me everything she saw, says she will once she's processed and can talk about it. All Vee will say is she'll stop what she saw from happening.

Most importantly, and to my relief, she tells me she felt powerful against Chaos.

"Did we help you?"

I wait, eager to hear anything that could guide us towards any clue. Darkness flickers across her face. "You were there, but don't ask me any more. I almost didn't tell anybody at all, but we can't hide things."

I want to say that she is hiding things, but I also understand how she sometimes doesn't deal with trauma. How much really changed in Vee? Is she hiding the girl we saw in the snow, that night in Scotland, the one hellbent on hunting Chaos and demons down? Or is she still precariously balancing between human and whatever she is now?

"I'm worried about what Logan said—the energy he saw. Can you sense it?" she asks, as if reading my mind.

"I think you're charged with more energy somehow,

through the four of us. Maybe our idea was right all along, and we activated something inside you."

Vee takes a ragged breath and I'm alarmed when her eyes well with tears. *Shit, not this again.* But I should be happy, because this emotional reaction means despite the visions, the teleporting and energy, she's still the Vee we love. A slightly drunk version, but Vee.

"A lot scares me right now, but one thing frightens me the most." She whispers. "If whatever I am needed to absorb power from each of you, and some kind of destiny is fulfilled, will you stop feeling for me as intensely? Will you still want me here? All of you, I mean."

If her fears were true, I wouldn't stand here and look at Vee with my heart hurting for her. If our relationship was only created to keep us close enough that she could take our energy, now I'd return to seeing her as a weapon, and know who against. Vee's not only a part of me because of this weird situation, but because I care about her. So fucking much.

"I don't understand what you mean, Vee. We're a team. All of us."

"If I'm this energy Logan saw though, I'm not your Vee, am I? What am I to you all now..."

Oh shit. Actual tears. I run a hand across my head and respond the only way I know how. If I hug Vee, comfort her, I can't see the tears and maybe I'll stop them. I wrap Vee in my arms, holding her head against my chest, willing her to stay calm. She doesn't feel any different to the last time I did this, she's still my Vee. Our Vee.

My aching heart races in response to her body close to mine, and I'm shocked by how sudden and intense the need for her is. I've noticed the tension crackling between her and the guys since she changed, realised what this means, but this is fucking overwhelming. We're not further apart after her absorbing our energy, we're closer.

Vee pulls her face away and looks up at me. Her reddened eyes have darkened as her response matches mine, her mouth parted as she looks back.

Oh hell.

I take Vee's face in both hands and mash my lips onto hers. She parts them eagerly, allowing my tongue to explore her mouth. Vee holds my head in return and kisses me with an intensity that makes every kiss between us before seem as if we held back.

I feel Vee, in my heart, in every cell, as if I can't be whole without her touch and kiss and this takes over. Not taking my mouth off hers, I back Vee to the kitchen counter and move to slide my hands beneath her top. She does the same, fingernails dragging across my lower back. I'm hard, and so fucking quickly it's insane. I can't get close enough, and she arches towards me as I press her into the bench with my hips.

Wrenching my mouth from hers, I look down, struggling to breathe. She looks back, pausing as I do. I trace my finger along her full lips. "Nothing's changed and won't change. Can't you feel the effect you have on me?"

"Physical," she murmurs and moves her hand to my crotch between us, and sends more pleasure through as her fingers brush my erection beneath.

"You know I mean more than physical," I whisper hoarsely. She needs to hear this. Vee needs to know. "You mean the same to me as you did two days ago." I brush my lips against hers, controlling myself, holding them in place and hoping she feels what I do.

Vee slides her hand upwards and places her palm against my heart, which thumps harder than ever. "In here?"

What do I say? If I tell Vee what I'm thinking, will she assume I'm saying the words because she wants to hear them?

"You know you're in there. I never had a chance at keeping you out."

Vee's answer is a hard kiss, one where our teeth collide and we're lost in each other. I struggle to hold back, but Vee's pulling me under. I slide my mouth away from hers again, struggling to hold on to my self-control. We're in the kitchen. Sure, the other guys went upstairs, but still. Bad idea.

"Don't stop," she whispers.

"You're drunk."

"No. Xander, I need this. I need to feel connected. I have to know I am."

I grab Vee by the hips and lift her onto the counter. We exist in our own space, out of time. As we hold each other's faces, the shared breath between us is hot and intense. The charge beneath our fingers where we touch cheeks, between our lips where they hover so close together, trips the switch on the energy between us and everything floods out.

This is the final surrender. A surrender to myself, not her. When I kiss her again, my soul splinters. The remaining parts I've held together are torn apart by the intense energy coming from Vee, and the relief I never lost her.

She pulls at my T-shirt and I help tug it over my head, her hands going straight to the button on my jeans. My body trembles with the desire to consume the girl who consumes me. I push her shirt upwards and kiss Vee's skin, exhaling out control as my stubbled cheek presses against her soft skin.

Vee feels the same, tastes the same, and her scent

engulfs as before. No. She's not the same; Vee's so much more to me now.

Vee tugs at my hair so I have to meet her eyes. I'm looking into a mirror, but not because I'm looking at the War in Vee's eyes. There is more spoken in this look we share than any kiss. This connection will never break.

"Aha!" A female voice comes from behind.

I drop Vee's top where I have it pushed up and close my eyes. "Hello, Syv."

"I'd say don't let me stop you, but you're kind of close to the sink and I want some water." She pokes her tongue out. "Feels like something crapped in my mouth."

This girl has no shame as she walks over, takes a glass from the drainer and proceeds to fill it. Vee stares at Syv, mouth parted, and I place my hands on the counter, either side of Vee.

"I find sex on kitchen counters uncomfortable. I mean, yeah, sometimes caught in the moment it happens, but ugh." She rubs her ass. "Y'know?"

If I can't believe the words coming out of Syv's mouth, I hate to think what Vee's thinking. I drag my T-shirt back over my head.

"Thanks for the advice," I half-growl.

"No problem." Syv sips her water. "Although, I'm glad you have your most of your clothes on, or this could've been awkward."

I look at Vee, relieved to see her fighting a smile. Really? Because this *is* bloody awkward and a huge mood killer.

"Night, kids." Syv winks at Vee and half-stumbles from the kitchen with her glass.

I rest my forehead against Vee and she giggles as she curls her hand around my head, playing with the hair at my nape. "For fuck's sake," I mutter.

She presses her lips on mine before kissing across my cheek to place them against my ear. "At least it was Syv and we were mostly clothed, rather than one of the guys and we were naked."

"True." I huff and step back, helping Vee from the counter.

"Besides." Vee gestures at the surroundings. "There's a lot that could get broken in here."

I smile and stroke her hair. "You mean with the literally earth-shattering orgasms I give you."

The smile Vee gives me fills my body with a warmth to match the day I watched her play in the snow. "If my changing also transforms you into the Xander who can joke with me, I can deal with that."

I tip my mouth into a half smile. "Hey, I'm not joking."

She runs a finger from my chest to the waistband of my jeans. "I know you're not."

How drunk is Vee? I've seen her worse, once, but right now I can't figure out if this is a good idea. It's taking all my self-control not to spin her around and fuck her against the kitchen counter.

Fuck, man. Calm down and think about where you are.

"We should go to bed," she whispers and tugs at my hand. "Be civilised for once."

Like a man held in a spell, I follow Vee upstairs, knowing full well if she walks into my bedroom, the self-control I'm hanging onto with my fingertips won't follow us in.

I hope bloody Syv didn't choose my bed.

My curtains are open, illuminating a Syv-free bed, and Vee stripping. The yellow moonlight highlights her curves as she pulls off her shirt and unclasps her bra, leaving me no choice but to put my hands and mouth on her.

Her long hair hides perfect pink nipples, waiting for me.

I gently trace my finger around the soft flesh. "You are so fucking gorgeous."

Dipping my head, I take her nipple into my mouth, sucking hard. A low sound in Vee's throat is accompanied by her arching herself closer. I tease her, running my tongue from her nipple, to the swell of her breast; around, then down, trailing my lips across every inch of her exposed skin.

She drops backwards on the bed, holding my head against her breasts, and I continue my slow exploration of her body. She's falling apart beneath my hands and mouth. I could easily fall too, cover Vee's heated body with mine. Perspiration slicks my forehead as I pull away from my concentration on her gorgeous tits and drag my shirt over my head. I hold her to me, and her smooth skin meets mine, nipples against my chest. Another small sound of arousal, and she presses against me, more urgently.

I'm startled by a noise outside, somewhere close to the house. Banging. I attempt to turn off the vigilance that curses me every day, and half-listen for one of the other guys to walk downstairs and check what the sound is, but nobody does.

Shit.

Vee's maddening touch and taste pull me away from my need to charge outside, but another noise stops me. A louder bang.

"It's probably Syv leaving," she murmurs and runs her fingers against my jeans, where my cock strains against them. "Xander. Please."

"Hang on."

"Omigod, no!" she hisses at me.

I'm a madman. A complete fucking idiot, and I curse that my power is my strongest drive, even stronger than this moment with Vee. I grab my T-shirt.

"I'll be a minute."

I kiss Vee briefly on the forehead and don't miss her sour and shocked look as I leave her.

As I walk through the door, I almost slam into Joss, walking from his room and rubbing bleary eyes. "Did you hear that noise?"

"Yeah." He runs a look along my body. "Having an exciting time, Xander?"

"Shut up. Come on." I pull on my T-shirt.

Joss shakes his head. "Go back to your fun. I'll take a look and call out if I sense or see anything. Could be Syv."

"That's what Vee said."

Joss's mouth curves into a smile. "Well, then."

Without another word, he jumps down the stairs two at a time. I pause, pulled in two directions. Trust Joss to sort this and go back to Vee, or help him.

No question.

Back in the room, Vee lies naked on the bed, head turned to one side as her tangled hair brushes her face. I move towards her, waiting for a word or movement, and as I get close I realise her heavy breathing isn't linked to the thought of me anymore.

Should I be insulted that I'm out of the door less than a minute and the girl in my bed passes out? Unable to resist, I sit and draw a line across her soft skin with a finger, looking down at how beautiful, how human and how amazing she is.

Refusing to be a creeper staring at her naked and asleep, I kiss Vee's cheek and pull a sheet over her body, then waver between staying and following Joss. Vee moves in her sleep, murmuring my name and asking where I am. She grips the sheet and her breathing speeds up. Mine does too, with panic she might be having another vision.

Screw it. Joss can deal. Vee needs me. I lie next to her and pull her into me. She lays her head on my chest and curls a slender arm across. I bury my nose into Vee's hair and my chest aches, stomach twisted in knots. I've denied there could be anything more than a crazy, physical need for each other, but that denial won't stand anymore.

I love Vee.

And from now on, I'm going to try bloody hard to show her.

9

Vee

Xander doesn't sleep late; he never does. This guy will never be the one who I'll spend lazy mornings in bed with. My head hurts—because of alcohol or teleporting? Probably both. By the time I pull myself downstairs for breakfast, Xander's out walking.

I eat toast, an ordinary act in the midst of this all. As I chew, I stare at my coffee cup, focusing on how I feel. Powerful? Yes. But the dark magic still haunts my thoughts.

I'm pissed off about last night with Xander and mortified I fell asleep. Seriously, how can I be on the verge of delicious things with the man finally showing me affection rather than brute sex and then slip into unconsciousness? That must've hit Xander right in the ego. I hope he wasn't in the room when I did. No, if he'd been touching me, my body would never have decided sleep was the way to go.

I blink as Syv storms into the room shouting for Xander, and an alarmed Joss appears too.

"What? What the fuck's happening? Is someone here?" Joss asks and looks around.

"Xander let my dog go!" she growls.

Joss's mouth falls open. "I thought you meant something bad had happened."

I chew my lip and look down. This girl is odd. Did Syv seriously think she could keep her weird animal?

"I didn't." Xander walks through the door and pulls his hood down. "I didn't go anywhere near the bloody thing."

"The door was open! Someone opened it." She snaps her head to Joss. "Was it you? Or Ewan?"

Xander crosses his arms. "I don't give a shit what happened. And I don't have time for your hysterics."

Joss touches Syv on the arm and she shakes him off. "He escaped, Syv. Me and Xander heard something last night and I went outside to investigate. The barn door was open and scratched. He's strong—must've broken the lock."

Her eyes widen and her mouth turns down. "Oh. Maybe he'll come back."

"Or maybe he'll find someone nice to eat," says Xander. He nods at me. "How are you feeling this morning, Vee?"

I flush red and drink my coffee. "Fine."

"Uh huh." He bites away a smile.

"Joss, did you find out what Spot is? Is he a hellhound?" continues Syv.

"Maybe. Not sure."

Xander straightens. "What?"

"The closest in appearance that Ewan could find is a hellhound."

My mouth dries, oh god, don't mention Hell again around Joss.

"Again, you should've killed the bloody thing!" Xander jabs a finger at Syv. "If it kills people, the blood is on your hands, Syv."

Out of everything in the world that's killing right now, Spot is low on the priority list. *Spot...*

"Look, forget this," puts in Joss. "Syv had something to say to me this morning over breakfast."

Over breakfast? Like we're a bunch of housemates chatting before heading out for the day.

All eyes turn to Syv, who scratches the side of her head. "Yeah, so you know how I work for different clients."

"By that you mean Ripley?" retorts Xander. "Yeah, we know."

"And the Collector," she adds. "He figured out where the book was from."

"Go on...."

"He called me back after you left that day and told me he knew who the book once belonged to. Col has an idea where the book was last kept before he acquired it. He pointed me in that direction, hoping there were items connected to the book we could use to decipher it. Maybe a parchment or a stone—something with runes to match the book."

"And he didn't tell us, why?" snaps Ewan.

"He's worried the book is dangerous; he wants to translate it himself. Besides, you were in Scotland."

"Syv! Why the fuck didn't you tell us?" asks Xander.

"I'm telling you now."

Ewan scowls at her. "I knew we couldn't trust you!"

"Hey! I'm on your side if you're allied with Ripley and the fae now."

"But is the Collector?"

Syv sighs. "He doesn't trust many people, so he's keeping

is distance, but he's okay with me talking to you guys. I was in Cambridge because Col suggested I look through certain collections there. I couldn't get close yesterday." She taps the table. "It's kinda one of the reasons for helping yesterday."

"Helping drink all the alcohol in the house?" says Joss with a laugh.

"You have no idea how stressful it is running from demons," she snaps.

"What?" Xander moves to sit next to her.

"They were following me, and now you've explained who Seth is, I know why I'm being followed. I'm no longer happy to do this shit on my own."

Heath and the others sit around the table with a guarded Syv, who gives a rundown on where she needs to go and what she needs to do.

There's no question—today we go to Cambridge.

10

Vee

Luckily, Cambridge isn't a long journey—we can visit and return in a day. Syv takes her car, and the rest of us travel in Heath's SUV. The mood is hopeful, but the tension still fills the air around us. What can we expect? I'm certain someone or something is looking for the item too, and finding out who could be a challenge.

We follow a group of school kids through the large doors into the museum's bright foyer. Syv wanted to arrive separately, so we join those milling around, also waiting for others or looking at maps and posters to plan their afternoon. Syv has favourite collections she checks out for artefacts and has pinpointed one based on her chat to the Collector. How many times has she visited the place and left with items she shouldn't? I'm surprised she's not on a 'banned' list.

The guys stand at strategic corners, watching the entry

and doors to other parts of the museum. I sit with Joss on the wood bench opposite the café, beneath the long windows, and rest my head on his shoulder. He's quiet again, and after the incident with the wraith, I'm paranoid every time Joss withdraws from us.

"You can tell me," I whisper.

"Tell you what?"

"If you've had any more weird memories." Joss shifts so my head isn't on him anymore and I look up, hurt. "Don't be like that."

He side-glances me, green eyes serious. "I can't talk. It's too distracting, Vee. I need to stay focused."

"What Seth said about God could be important. We need to persuade Xander to listen. You're all named after Biblical figures—it's not a hard connection to make."

He clenches his hands together in his lap and watches as a gaggle of school kids, holding hands in pairs, wander by. "They're what's important." He nods to them. "People. If something else comes up in the research that confirms Seth's story, I'll deal with what this could mean then."

"Okay. I understand." I pull one of his hands into mine and try to enclose it between my palms. "I worry about you all, especially you and Heath right now."

Joss gives me a half-smile before tipping my chin up with two fingers. "And that makes everything better. If you worry, you're still the Vee that loves us all."

"Nuclear Vee," I whisper with a laugh I don't feel like giving. I've an uncomfortable feeling I'll soon know what this energy is for, and a large part of me doesn't want to.

"No, *our* Vee." He kisses me softly on the mouth.

Someone coughs close by. "Can you guys not keep your hands off her?"

I look up. A woman with bobbed blonde hair and a

pink-painted mouth looks at us over a pair of large sunglasses she has pushed down her nose. The look isn't familiar, but the voice is.

"Syv?" asks Joss.

She winks. "As you can imagine, I'm known to security. I often pay visits to the same places when I acquire things I need."

Joss laughs and repeats 'acquire'.

I smile. "Blonde suits you."

Syv adjusts her hair. "Thank you. I didn't feel like the black one today." She twirls around and her knee-length floral skirt floats around her. "Don't I look cute!"

Joss shakes his head and points at her boots. "Doc Martens?"

"Hey, I never know when I'll need to kick someone. Or..." She opens the large, brown handbag hanging across one shoulder wide enough for me to see, and I look inside. A large knife. Of course.

Heath and Xander appear behind her, but Ewan remains close to the entrance. "Nice look," says Xander. "Wig looks a bit false though."

Syv pokes her tongue out at him.

Heath glances up at the CCTV camera. "We're walking into the ground floor displays first. Where are you going first, Syv?"

"I'm not sure if what we need is on display or in storage. My research showed what we're looking for is in a newer collection."

"Do you know exactly what you *are* looking for Syv?" asks Joss.

"An item that's part of this collection which has runes to match the book." Syv thrusts a museum brochure at him. "I've marked on there where to meet me. I'll see you there in thirty minutes. Please don't all follow at once; you know how attention-grabbing you are."

"Hopefully not something you need to drag through the museum." Joss smiles.

"In my experience, this will be a relic or parchment. Easy to fit in my bag." She taps the side. "Can I go?"

Xander reads and nods, and with a little wave, Syv heads away.

Walking through the museum unsettles me, as I'm pulled in by the thoughts that this is a world I've never belonged to. The echoing rooms fill with thousands of years of human history—a world Chaos wants destroyed. I'm flanked by Joss and Ewan; Ewan warily watching those around, and Joss occasionally stopping with genuine curiosity at displays.

Xander and Heath follow Syv at a distance, and we all watch for suspicious behaviour amongst the busy museum-goers. Ewan almost trips over another child who stops abruptly in front of him.

He swears under his breath. "This place is crawling with kids."

"School trips to the museum," I say and smile. "I enjoyed them."

Joss and Ewan exchange a look. *At least, my false memories think I did.*

"Whatever," mutters Ewan. "Seen anything yet?"

Joss indicates a sign on the wall. "Syv's headed to the room with one of the older civilisations to check there. I haven't seen anyone follow her, apart from Xander and Heath."

"Egypt?" Ewan asks.

"Nah, Mesopotamia."

Ewan looks at him as if he's speaking a foreign language. "Sure. Whatever."

"We're not expecting Seth, are we?" We walk towards the next doorway, shoes squeaking on the tiles amongst the hubbub around.

"No. We know Seth sends others to attack usually; he likes to play with us. The creatures in the car park. Joss's wraith." Joss tenses at Ewan's words. "So, we need to be really vigilant because we don't know what's next. I think, if anything, he'll send a lackey to try and intercept. Syv already said she's being followed."

I rest against a handrail looking over a re-creation of a Roman house. "Does Seth exist in history?"

"He's in a lot of religions. I looked him up after he revealed himself. Seth took his name from the Egyptian Chaos god, Set, although he's much older than that. He could just have easily chosen Roman, Greek, Celt...anything."

"Don't talk as if he has any right to be in human history. Chaos won't be anything by the time we've finished with him," growls Ewan before stomping away. People watch as he barges through them.

Joss wraps a strong arm around my shoulder, guiding me after Ewan. "Wow. Well that outburst came from nowhere. Do you reckon Xander will let us stop at the gift shop on the way out of the museum?"

"You say the weirdest things, Joss."

"Sometimes weird is the best way to cope." He raises his voice. "Ewan! Wait up."

Ewan pauses and looks over his shoulder at us.

"Don't be upset," Joss calls. "I'll buy you a dinosaur at the gift shop, but don't lose him before we get home like you did last time."

I fight laughing because Ewan strides back, face thunderous. "Stop shouting, do you want to draw attention to the fact we're here?"

Two boys nearby nudge each other before whispering and laughing.

"Yeah, I do. I'd rather anybody who's watching notices us and not Syv."

Ewan sighs and unfolds the museum map again. "Let's head after the others."

XANDER

Alongside Heath, I shadow Syv as she works her way through the crowds, slowly wandering from room to room. She pauses occasionally to look at an exhibit or check her phone, so we do the same.

I sigh and cross my arms as I stare at stuffed representations of animals from the Ice Age, or whatever. Two kids push in front of me, holding clipboards and pencils as they write notes. I step back and crane my neck to locate Syv, just as a gang with a teacher surge forward. I'm sick of bloody children today.

"Where did Syv go?" I ask Heath.

"No idea."

"What the hell?" I growl.

He looks around too. "She doesn't want us close—maybe she went to the lower floor. Where're the nearest stairs?"

My phone beeps and I look down.

<Not on display. Checking store rooms. Ground floor. Back of building. Check map.>

I blow air into my cheeks as I read Syv's words. She should've waited. A blue circle on my map shows where she marked the spot earlier, and we head in the direction.

Syv's mentioned she's familiar with the room that stores the items entering or leaving the museum for displays. This is her usual first place to look; often items are borrowed from other institutions, or used for research, and are never placed out on the museum floor.

We make our way to the top of the stairs to wait. "I'll text the others and ask them to meet us there." Heath's hair flops into his face as he focuses on his phone.

A girl pauses and stares up at me; I frown down at her. What does she want? I hazard a guess she's a teen, perhaps a year or two younger than Elyssia, and wears a maroon and black uniform with a white shirt. Brown hair, big blue eyes, unsure smile. I don't smile back, hoping she moves on.

"Hi," she says.

"Hey." I look past her for Ewan and Joss.

"I lost my children."

"Uh?" I turn my eyes to hers. Surely, she doesn't have kids.

"Oh! I mean the two I'm supervising. Girls. Both brown hair. I swear they gave me the worst kids to supervise. I've had nothing but attitude all day. I'm in trouble if I don't find them—because they're bound to be doing something wrong."

"Right." Why the hell is she asking me? Do I look like a responsible adult? Maybe she's a demon or someone sent by Seth to distract us. I study her closer and immediately stop when the girl's cheeks turn pink under my scrutiny. "How old?"

"I'm seventeen." She pauses and her big eyes widen. "Shit. I mean whoops. Crap. No, you meant the kids, didn't you?"

Heath snickers next to me, and I rub my temples. Awkward. "I did. Are they dressed like you? Same school?"

"It's okay. Sorry to bother you." The poor girl has turned a shade redder and she scurries away.

"Ah, Xander, you never fail to impress, do you?" Heath says with a laugh.

"I was only standing here!"

A hand clasps my shoulder and I jerk, ready to retaliate, and meet Ewan's curious face. "What are you doing? Who's she?"

"Doesn't matter." I keep an eye on her, and when she approaches someone dressed in a museum uniform, I relax. "Syv wants to meet us here." I point at the map. "Next floor down. Should we all go?"

Joss holds up a hand to silence me and then strides along the hallway a few metres. He returns with a worried look. "Vee? Can you feel that? I swear I can sense a demon."

She frowns as he takes her arm and leads her further down the hallway. Vee folds her arms and they speak too quietly for us to hear before returning.

"Was it the girl, do you think?" asks Ewan.

"Maybe?" suggests Vee.

"Shit!" I pause. "No. I don't think so."

"She didn't distract you to let someone else past?"

"Nah, I was in front of the stairs."

"Typical bloody Syv, heading off alone," I mutter.

"Because she normally works alone." Ewan shoves hands in his pockets and looks around. "But I thought she'd be more worried about being followed, now she knows about Seth."

"I'm sure she isn't far."

"Text her." I wave a hand at Ewan. "Head downstairs and see if she's there."

"I think two of us should wait at the museum entrance," puts in Joss. "I'm worried we might miss something."

I rub my mouth. He's right. "Okay. Take Vee. Ewan?"

He shrugs. "I can hang around the entrance again, if you want. Take Heath."

Plan made, we head in our different directions. I curse Syv under my breath. Okay, she can look after herself, but she's not taking seriously how much threat she's under here.

"Heath—downstairs. Come on."

11

Vee

Joss halts by the gift shop and tugs on Ewan's arm, repeating his joke about dinosaurs. Ewan is as unimpressed as last time. The tables at the café close to the entrance are emptier and I toy with the idea of a takeaway coffee. I'm surprised Xander didn't stop to inspect the menu earlier, while we waited for Syv to arrive.

"I'm heading to the bathroom before we go. The excitement is too much." I grin at my attempt at light humour, but neither respond. With a sigh, I indicate the bathroom signs and head off. "Buy Ewan his dinosaur while I'm gone."

I edge around children now assembling to leave, but the door is locked with a "closed for cleaning" sign. I glance back to the guys but they're deep in conversation. How far to the next bathrooms?

An announcement sounds—the museum will close in half an hour. I hope I don't spend ten minutes trawling around trying to find another bathroom. I take the next set of stairs down to the lower floor and walk towards the bathroom sign.

The corridor is narrow with no doors apart from a fire exit leading out at the opposite end and the bathrooms, but a right turn a few metres away presumably leads to other areas on this level of the museum.

I sense something.

From inside the bathrooms?

I slowly push open the heavy door and peek in. Two little girls stand at the sinks and splash each other with water, giggling as they do. The school-uniformed pair stop and straighten, caught in the act as they look at me. How old are they? Maybe twelve? I can never tell.

"Shouldn't you be with your school friends?" I ask, attempting my strictest voice.

They blink back at me.

"Where's your group? Surely a teacher should be supervising you."

One clears her throat. "We needed to pee. What's it to you?"

"The museum is closing. I suggest you go now before you get into trouble." My stern tone continues.

With a silent and haughty look, the girls snatch their schoolbags from the floor and stalk past me. I watch them go as the door bangs closed. Wow, attitude. I'm glad I don't have kids to deal with.

Aware I'm short of time too, I head into a stall. I've barely time to lock the door when the main bathroom door crashes open.

"Get the fuck off me!" snaps a voice I recognise.

"Simple. Give me that stone."

My mouth dries as I peer through the gap between the door and cubicle wall. Syv. Tall man. He has her cornered near the sink that the girls stood at a few minutes ago.

"Yeah. Nah." Syv strikes out, her elbow collides with his face, and she attempts to duck beneath his arm. The man barely flinches and, with one hand, slams her by the chest against the tiles. The sudden, pained expression is quickly replaced by a narrow-eyed disgust.

"Dude..." She jerks her knee upwards, colliding with his balls, but again he doesn't flinch. Syv laughs dryly. "Wow, impressive."

What do I do? I'm seconds from stepping out and dealing with the situation when I see a knife blade flash. He spins Syv around and presses it against her throat.

"I know you're here." He outstretches a leg and I back away as he kicks open the door, the lock splintering. "Get out."

Even before I saw him, I knew this guy was a demon. He reeks of it and his appearance doesn't do him any favours. Tall and gangly with a face covered in livid scars, including one slicing across his mouth.

I catch the door before it hits me and I straighten. He's not touching me. "Let Syv go."

His eyes narrow. "Are you a lowlife friend of hers?"

I smile. "You have no idea, do you?"

As I talk, Syv delves into her large bag, looking straight ahead to avoid the knife nicking her skin. Why doesn't she look terrified? He has a knife against her jugular. The man stares at me and his eyes blacken.

"I know the Horsemen are here," he replies. "They shouldn't send someone weak to do their dirty work."

"I'm not weak," retorts Syv.

"Sure, sweetheart. I don't see you escaping me. I could slash your throat in an instant."

"You won't get a chance," I say. "You hurt her, and the Horsemen will rip you to shreds."

"Yeah, then where are they?"

I fight a smile and say the words I've itched to use. "Don't you know who I am?"

He looks me up and down and squeezes Syv tighter against himself.

"Not someone who could take me on. The guy who paid me to do this gave me some extra juice—I'm stronger than the pair of you together."

"I doubt that." I mutter, then add, "Let me guess, the man who paid you to do this calls himself Seth."

The demon blinks rapidly. "He's more than just a name."

"So am I."

"So, what is your name, sweetheart?"

Before I can reply, Syv pulls a large stone from her bag and smacks the guy across the face with it. He howls and drops his grip, fingers going to his nose.

"You wanted the stone," she says with a smirk and takes advantage of his distraction to step away.

Me and the guy stare at the grey, half-tablet clasped in Syv's hand. The edges are cracked and the surface etched.

She found what we needed.

Regaining his senses, the demon grabs Syv again and puts the knife to her throat. "Stupid move."

As the knife cuts her skin, Syv drops the stone and claws at his fingers. My stomach turns, aware what's about to happen and I freeze, not knowing what the hell to do. Magic flies from my hands, black sparks arcing across the space between us . The demon screams in pain and drops the knife—and Syv—before sinking to the floor, holding his head.

What the hell? I didn't conjure that—I had no thought about magic in my mind, I was about to call on my strength to take him on.

Syv watches in alarm, hand across her neck, as the demon doesn't move from the floor, then she snatches the knife. The darkness continues to swirl around his figure, wrapping his body like rope. What the fuck? Heath's magic is bright, like lightning bolts, and mine can blind.

This is pure darkness.

"Holy shit, dude," breathes out Syv as she watches the crackling bonds pull tighter around him. His face reddens, and he uselessly tries to pull the magic wrapping away. The magic winds further and further, quicker and quicker.

The door behind begins to open and Syv steps past, slamming her back against it. Someone on the other side attempts to push again. "Hello?" A woman's voice. "What's happening?"

Uh, well, we're killing a demon and my friend just stole something from the museum. "Nothing!" I call back.

"Why's the door stuck?"

"I'm trying to open it now," says Syv and glances back at me, lowering her voice. "Sort him out." She points at the demon.

The choking, shaking mess on the floor grows closer to death and I push both hands into my hair. How exactly do the Horsemen deal with inconvenient bodies when they kill in public?

"I don't know how."

"Oh, fucking great." Syv slams her back harder against the door. "What does that magic do? Will it disintegrate him or something?"

"I've never used it before. It's new since..." I stare down at my palms. Darkness. Is this part of Chaos's power? The room lurches and I steady myself on the sink. No. I can't have his too.

"Since you changed?"

"Hello?" calls the voice. "Can you open the door, before we get security."

Syv mutters "shit" over and over under her breath and gestures with her free hand. "Try and do something. Seriously, with my bleeding neck, I don't think we'd be able to explain this away."

Blood seeps between her fingers. Shit. How bad is she? I rub both hands down my face and close my eyes. I've only seen Seth summon lightning bolts from the sky, which is no use in this situation. Ewan mentioned Seth created a black void. Can I do that?

Tears prick my eyes. I don't want to attempt to copy anything Seth did, because it's proof I somehow contain Chaos's powers too. Contain *him*.

"Vee!" urges Syv.

Heart racing, I hold a palm in front of me and imagine the void that swirled towards me in Ewan's room the night I changed.

The darkness I can no longer deny lives inside me.

The view between me and the bathroom sinks obscures, as all colour disappears. An intense cold enters the room as the black void before me grows, spreading the way the portal did. But this is different. This feels like a hole in the fabric of the world, hovering above the demon's body. I step forward and look at the now-immobile man. At least he's dead before whatever happens next. What am I sending him to?

The growing black, with pinprick stars behind, grows

around the demon, moving away from me and swallowing his figure. Syv says something behind me, but I don't hear her words, totally fixated on the scene in front of me. I can't see him anymore, just the absent part of the bathroom, as if I painted it away.

My body jerks as the darkness snaps to a small circle in front of me, and I'm pushed back onto the floor, landing on my ass. The demon has gone. I gasp for breath as a white light pushes forward, and this time when I stare at my hands the familiar glow from my magic has returned, obliterating the dark.

"Vee!" Syv moves away from the door and crouches down. I shake as I stare at my fingers. My chest hurts, the pain growing in my head too; a pressure as if I'm fighting a migraine. I blink around at Syv, who stretches out her fingers before withdrawing and covering her mouth.

The door slams open and a middle-aged woman in a museum uniform frowns down at me. "What happened?"

"I didn't feel well," I croak out.

"She collapsed in front of the door," says Syv. "I just moved her."

"Are you okay? Does she need first aid?" Her anger turns to a troubled look and she barely glances at Syv.

"I'm fine now." I attempt a smile.

"Her nose is bleeding." She looks to Syv. "Do you have tissues in your bag?"

"I like to carry the essentials." Syv smiles through her pale shock and delves into her bag. *Yeah, like a knife. Stolen artefacts.*

"What happened to your neck?" The woman points at where the demon began to slice into Syv, and I stare in alarm at the amount of blood. How far from an artery was he?

"I really think I should get someone," the woman says. "Stay there." Without waiting for our response, she rushes from the room.

"Shit. We need to go. Can you walk?" Syv crouches down and offers me a tissue.

Taking hold, I nod and press it against my nose. She helps me stand on my shaky legs. "Your neck."

Syv touches her skin and looks at the blood on her fingers. "I'm good. I'll head to the hospital to get it fixed up; I've had worse. Two secs."

She produces a black scarf from her bag and tightens it around her neck. "Fashionable and practical."

Wow. "You're certainly prepared!"

"It's bleeding a lot though, isn't it?"

"I might be able to help," I suggest as I straighten my clothes and follow to the door.

"With that dark shit?" Syv arches a brow. "That's not the kind of magic I want touching me."

"I wouldn't—" I begin to retort, but Syv winks at me. "Fine. Come on."

Turning my head, I catch sight of myself in the mirror: the pale-faced girl with a tissue held over her nose.

Bile rises as I see my eyes. I don't know whose they are, but they don't look like mine. I squeeze them shut as Syv grabs my hand. "Quick! Where did you leave the guys?"

"Do my eyes look strange?" I ask her.

"No." I glance back at the mirror. They're back to the same green as usual but hold the fear I feel.

Syv succeeds in dragging me from the bathrooms and in the opposite direction to the stairs I came down. We break through the fire door and an alarm sounds.

"Fucking love this part!" Syv runs ahead, hand on her neck, and lifts up her other arm. She waves the grey stone at me. "I found what we needed—a stone. Mission accomplished. Kinda."

Kinda?

12

JOSS

I wince as Xander drops into one of his rants, yelling across the kitchen at Syv, Vee, and anybody who dares interrupt him.

He barely said two words in the car on the way back. Vee, sensibly, accompanied Syv to avoid talking to him if she'd travelled with us.

I don't know what the fuck happened at the museum. We found the pair in the car park. Eventually. They drove up in Syv's Jeep, yelling at us to follow them before anybody saw. What had been annoyance turned to relief that they weren't stuck in the back of the museum somewhere or had been seriously injured.

But even in the streetlight's glow, I saw blood on Syv's neck, soaking the top of her dress. There was blood around Vee's nose and I was terrified they'd met Seth. Apparently not—but obviously whoever the guy they met is, he worked for someone else looking for the stone. So, yeah, probably Seth.

Now, back at the house, the demanding questions begin.

"All I did was go to the bathroom," says Vee, facing off Xander, arms crossed. "We didn't exactly have time to call for the cavalry when the guy attacked Syv."

"She's right, Xander," I say. "Vee didn't sneak off. She told us where she was going."

"They should never have let you go alone." Xander's eyes narrow. "We'd promised not to because of the fucking teleporting thing."

I sigh. "Xan. Come on. Calm down."

"If there had been more than one of us with Syv, the situation might not have happened." He turns to jab a finger at Syv. "Why the fuck didn't you wait for us?"

"Because I saw somebody else hanging around, near the store room, who I knew wasn't human. I had to get in and take the stone before he could."

Xander glowers. "You could've waited. We weren't far behind."

"And what if he'd walked off with it while I did? Let me do my job, Xander. Everything worked out okay."

"Only because Vee was there. Someone could've found you on the floor with your throat slashed."

Syv steps toward him. "Plenty have tried, and nobody has succeeded. I would've got myself out of the situation. Eventually."

Xander yanks out a kitchen chair and sits beside Ewan. "What's your opinion?"

"What happened to the demon's body?" he asks in a low voice.

My suspicion piques as Vee and Syv exchange a glance. "What are you hiding?"

"She obliterated the dude. That's all," Syv replies. "Joss, are you gonna fix my neck up or should I head to Emergency? I don't mind, there's a cute doctor there who's often working."

I shake my head and pull out the first aid kit from a cupboard.

"Obliterated? Full story, Vee. Now." Xander folds his hands under his arms. Vee's mouth thins at Xander's attitude to her. "Please," he adds.

The demon was strong, if Syv couldn't take him. Her magic powers may be weak, but I've said before, her physical ability comes from more than human strength.

Vee hesitantly tells us about the magic, but I swear she downplays the scene. A dark power? Okay, she used this on a demon, but it was a triggered reflex. What does that mean for the future?

"Can we talk about the stone that Syv found?" she asks eventually. "This must be what we need as the symbols look familiar. That's what's important here. Show them, Syv."

The stone Syv took from the museum is on the table between us. Flat, grey, with a few runes carved on both sides.

Broken.

"Why is there blood on it?" Ewan picks up the stone and examines it.

"I hit the bastard with it." She winces as I prod at her cut. "Careful, Doctor Famine."

"I think Steri-Strips should be okay." I delve into the box.

"What did you need to tell us?" Heath takes the stone and runs his finger along the rough edge. "It's broken, isn't it?"

"Looks that way. Clean break. I think someone took the other part elsewhere."

"Oh, for fuck's sake!" Heath drops the stone. "Where?"

Syv reaches into her back pocket and pulls out a sheet of paper. She spreads it on the table in front of her as I attach the surgical tapes to her neck. "This was in the drawer with the stone. It's a shipment record. The stone and other items are on loan from the Louvre museum in Paris. I think that's where the other part might be."

"Shit!" Xander stands and kicks the chair back under the table. "What if Seth has that stone already?"

"The demon has been following me, so I doubt he knows where he's going without me leading him there. Maybe if the demon had taken this, Seth would know." She taps the paper. "But he didn't. I did what I'm paid for."

"So now we need to go to fucking Paris?" Ewan's face sours. "We can't all go there and leave this place unprotected."

"Yeah, and we need to keep an eye on Ripley," puts in Heath.

"Well, we're not splitting up." Xander takes the paper. "Are you sure the stone is in that museum?"

"No. But it's a good guess," replies Syv. "I'm willing to look."

"You could ask the Collector to go with you." I look in surprise at Vee's suggestion to Syv. "You said he has strong magic."

Syv plays her fingers over the wound-closing strips I've put on her skin. "Maybe. Why? Don't you trust me to go alone?"

"You need protecting, look at what just happened."

"S'pose."

Vee closes her hand over Syv's and I'm surprised when

Syv doesn't withdraw it. "I just saw what happened, Syv. If he can't go, one of us will need to."

"Not happy about that," mumbles Xander.

"Let me talk to Col. I promised I'd head back to him as soon as we'd finished up in Cambridge." She gives a half smile. "He worries about me, y'know."

Beneath her words, I sense a different sentiment. Syv likes that someone cares about her. This girl isn't the flirtatious assassin with an attitude as big as her knives. I'm unsure if the guys see past her front, but I do. I figured her out early on, and the more time we're around Syv, the more I see who she hides beneath. She pretends not to give a shit but I sense she's lost in the world too.

"Do you want us to come with you to the Collector's?" I ask as I tidy the bloodied gauze into a pile.

"All good. It's a short drive. I'll be fine."

As Syv leaves, Vee follows. I walk to the lounge and watch out the window. They pause by her Jeep, chatting. Syv places a hand on Vee's shoulder and for a weird moment I think they might hug.

They don't. Vee walks back to the house as Syv drives away, and as the light from the open front door catches her expression, her pale-faced worry shines back at me.

13

VEE

Syv's chat to the Collector goes well, which surprises us. The reclusive fae must be worried if he's stepping in to help out. Or is his concern for Syv? The decision is made; Syv and the Collector head to Paris to follow her lead—he can protect her, and we can keep our fingers crossed the Louvre is the correct place. I could tell the guys were split between wanting to go with her and staying here. The decision we stick together as much as possible, and as closely as possible, is made. They toyed with the idea half our group could go, but Paris is too far apart for us all right now.

We're counting on a couple of days at the most. Syv and the Collector left straightaway the next morning, and both want to be there and back as quickly as possible.

I walk into the lounge where Xander and Heath stand together, jackets on, and halt. "Where are you going?"

"A night away from crazy shit. We can't do anything else until Syv and the Collector find what we need. Seth is quiet, probably watching them, so I've persuaded Xander to take a night off." Heath pokes his brother.

"Let me guess. Pub?"

"Not a total night off," he says gruffly. "We can check out the local area in case any supes are taking advantage of our distraction and are up to no good."

Heath chuckles. "Check out the bars, more like."

"Warehouse, La Fee Verte, or the King's Arms?"

"Why not just have a pub crawl?" I ask and snicker. "Enjoy."

I make to walk past to the kitchen and Heath stops me with a hand. "Aren't you coming?"

"Do I translate that as 'you're coming with us'?"

"Vee might not want to go. We can go somewhere more interesting if you want, Vee?" Joss walks into the room. "'We' as in me and you."

"We stick—"

"—together." I finish Xander's sentence for him. "I know."

"Aww, so no date with Vee?" Joss pouts.

I pat his cheek. "No special treatment for you today. Maybe another time."

"What are you talking about?" Ewan appears and flops down in his chair, feet on the table.

"We're going out, apparently," I tell him.

"Oh? I'm not."

"Yes, you are," Xander replies.

"No. I'm not. I'm going for a ride later, now the snow has melted. I want to clear my head a bit." Ewan leans forward and switches on the TV.

"You know? You're right," I say. "I'd like to forget about some of this for a few hours. Is that okay? How about The

King's Arms? I haven't been there since the day Heath took me to meet his smoking hot friends and a guy called Fay tried to kill me."

Stony expressions look back at me.

"Come on, guys! I'm trying to do what you're saying. Switch off. Down time."

Pretend to be human.

"It's quieter than the Warehouse or fae joint," suggests Joss. "Ewan, you can ride there if you want. Do both."

"Yeah. Maybe." He flicks through to a music channel.

"We're leaving." Xander picks Heath's car keys up from the table and throws them at Heath. "You're driving."

"Huh? Isn't it your turn?" Heath throws them back at him.

"Nope." The keys pass between them again and Heath scowls.

With a sigh, Joss grabs his keys. "I'll drive. Vee? Are you coming?"

I glance at Ewan. We need to talk. "Maybe I'll persuade Ewan to join you. He can take me on his bike again."

Ewan tips his head upwards and back onto the sofa. "You don't like my bike."

"You said that last time. Maybe I want to try again."

Joss chuckles. "We'll expect you in a couple of hours, then."

"I'm not going for that long a ride."

"Yeah, but we all know what happens when you two are left alone in the house."

Ewan looks around to the TV again, and I pull a face at Joss. "I'm going to change. See you there," I tell him.

With everything happening, a night out feels weird, but I understand why. There's little we can do until Syv appears with the other half of the stone. All we can do is monitor events in the world and hope Seth's leaving his plans until he has the information we're seeking too. A few hours won't hurt; besides, Ewan's bound to spend time on his phone watching for anything suspicious.

I return downstairs dressed in jeans and a shirt. Ewan flicks a look the length of me before pointing. "Are you stealing my shirt again?"

I'm wearing the oversized black shirt over a tight black tank top. The material slips down my arm as I lift the sleeve to my face and smile. "I like this shirt. It smells of you."

He doesn't respond, so I cross to sit next to him on the sofa. Ewan shuffles along but I move closer to him and he keeps his attention on the TV.

I pick up the remote and switch off the music. "You're avoiding me again, aren't you, Ewan?"

He turns wary eyes to mine. "Are you surprised after what happened last time we uh... had sex?"

"I don't think that will happen again. You know that was linked to you being the last guy I had sex with." He blinks at my bluntness and continues to watch me doubtfully. "Didn't you enjoy it, Ewan?"

"What do you think? Of course I bloody did, but it's difficult to cope with the girl I love freaking out and running away afterwards, possessed by an unknown force."

He frowns when I laugh. "Sorry, but that sounds very dramatic."

"It's true, Vee." His face hardens. "And you're different. We can all feel it."

I run my fingers down his cheek. "But the human Vee is containing the power still. It's stronger, but I'm in control of myself." Or I hope I am. Whatever triggered the darker magic yesterday wasn't under my control. Please let that only happen when I'm around demons—but please not Ripley.

"The change is making all our feelings stronger." He catches my hand and kisses my fingers. "I'm damn sure we're all trying hard to keep our hands off you. Most of us are succeeding, but it's not easy."

I sigh. "Ewan, you overthink everything. So what if you all don't keep your hands off me? I'm happy and everybody accepts it. It's just part of...this."

He chews on his lip and stares at his hands.

Oh.

"Are you saying you don't accept it?" I ask.

"No. Yes. I mean, I feel like with me, sex must be different, and I screwed this up."

"No." I hold his face in both hands and look back into his eyes. His confusion matches what I've seen before, when I want to see the love and desire. "You didn't."

"Yeah, well, I never had a girl react to me like that before." He half smiles and I push down the jealous twinge. What do other girls matter now?

"I'm sorry. I promise I won't next time." I kiss his cheek and he turns away. "Ewan! Honestly, you're pissing me off. Are you still angry with me about Seth?"

"Angry? I was never angry. Frustrated, maybe."

"I'm annoyed with myself for trusting Seth and not listening to you all. I felt a strong need to defend him and keep him close, and now he's gone I don't know why I did. I honestly can't figure why I trusted him so fully." I pause. "Do you think Seth had the ability to influence my thoughts?"

Ewan eyes me warily. "You won't want to hear this, Vee, but I think you contain part of his power too."

Ewan's words hit me in the gut. I've denied this thought

whenever it crossed my mind. But the darkness. The void I conjured. "What do you mean?"

"I'm convinced part of what he is, is inside you. And if you're linked to him, that's why you reacted the way you did."

I shift away. "That isn't true! He's barely touched me."

"You had part of us inside before we touched you. We just made it stronger when we did"

My stomach turns. "Do you think he'd try to..." *Omigod.* "He wouldn't. I'd fucking kill him first."

"Which is why I think you're here: to kill him. He's scared of you, I'm sure."

"Good. Maybe this mysterious book has a spell or something—anything—to help us. Do you think?"

Ewan shrugs. "But I'm fucking terrified. Okay, you never disappeared afterwards the way I thought you might, but I almost don't want to know what's in that book."

I take a deep breath. "Me either. But we need to."

"Yeah." He runs his fingers across my cheeks and lips, his mouth turned down. "I don't care what happens to me, but you...it would kill me if something happened to you."

'Something happened'? The words aren't spoken but I know what he's saying. If I die.

"Remember the time we sat together before, alone in the house? You said we can only live in the present. We should do that."

Ewan rubs his lips together, and his shining eyes show he's having the memory of our time on the sofa when we were interrupted. "What we did together that night, or what I said?"

"Both." I move my face closer and brush my lips against his cheek. This time he doesn't move away. Our faces touch and his stubble prickles me, sending a wave of memories through. He's right about the intensity. If I'm alone with any of the guys, my heart starts racing. If I'm physically close, the need to connect swamps my thoughts.

And I know Ewan's the same right now. His breathing picks up and he digs his fingers into the back of my hair. "I can't stay away however hard I try."

"You always told me that."

We stay in the moment, cheeks against each other, and I know if I slide my mouth to meet his, we'll take the extra time to leave that Joss predicted.

"We don't have to stay away from each other. I want us to be together, Ewan. I need to show you how much you mean to me, and that this time things will end differently."

We press closer together and his heart thumps against my chest. The grip on my hair tightens and I wait for him to make the move, because I refuse to. I need to know this is what he wants.

But disappointment replaces the lust running through my body as he releases my hair and sinks back.

"We should join the others." He runs a trembling hand through his hair as he looks ahead.

Rejecting me.

I swallow and stare at the side of his face. "You're hurting me, Ewan."

Dark eyes meet mine. "I hurt you last time. Can you understand how that makes me feel? Please? What if this time something worse happens?"

My frustration bubbles over and I stand, stomach in knots. "For fuck's sake, Ewan. This is stupid. If you don't want to be around me, fine. I'll call Joss and he can pick me up."

Heart hurting, I move away to find my phone, fighting the tears pricking my eyes after his rejection.

"Vee." Ewan's low voice comes from behind, and he wraps his arms around my waist, mouth touching the back of my neck.

*E*WAN

The moment I saw the hurt in Vee's eyes, my resolve dropped away and the need to show her how she makes me feel takes over from my fear. I'm telling the truth—I *am* scared. I'm terrified what I might do to her.

This woman tears me apart. Vee has no clue about the power she holds over me. Every time her soft lips meet mine, each time the taste and scent of her surges through with a kiss, Vee destroys me further. I crave her, I need the rush she gave me before, and I'm prepared to chase the high at any cost.

The lust pushes away the fear, and her hurt prevents me dwelling on the past. She's right. We know nothing of the future and can only be part of now.

Fuck it.

I spin Vee around and seize her face in both hands. She stumbles as I claim her mouth. Vee immediately responds, gripping my head in return and not holding back. We don't pause as the desire and understanding pours between us, each touch and kiss pulling us back to the place we want to be. Together, away from all the insanity surrounding us.

I grip Vee's hair and pull her head back, and her pulse races against my lips as I move them across her neck. Vee's body is soft and yielding, her scent intoxicating, and I can't keep the control I promised myself.

I don't want that control anymore.

I move my mouth back to Vee's and roughly part her lips with my tongue, my fingers moving to unbutton her shirt. There's no protest from Vee, instead she helps with trembling fingers and drops the shirt to the floor.

The lust takes over again and I press Vee against the wall. "I want you so fucking much. I lied when I said I didn't."

She looks back, eyes dark and cheeks flushed. "I know."

I'm desperate to touch and inhale the scent of Vee's skin, and to be back in the time and place we were lost before, to bring that from the past to now. Unbuttoning her jeans, I yank at the material and she wriggles until they slide downwards. She smiles back at me, cheeks flushed.

In response, she drags my T-shirt over my head and runs featherlight fingers across my pecs to my hard abs and downwards to my waistband. Vee moves her hand between us and brushes her fingers against my bulging cock as our mouths meet again. She deftly undoes my fly, her hand curling around my length as I shuffle my jeans and briefs to the floor.

Fuck. I wanted the next time with Vee to be slow and loving, but there's no chance of that.

I lift Vee and slide my hands across her smooth skin as she tightens her legs around my waist. I push myself close, my cock hardening against her thin panties. Vee grasps me around the neck and my mouth closes over hers, our kiss fevered as we tangle tongues.

I taste and relish Vee's sweetness, the first step towards showing her everything she means—and does—to me.

Vee moans into my mouth and I press harder against her. She arches towards me and I slide my hands up her sides, pulling her bra downwards to slide my tongue against her breast's soft mound. As I close my mouth over her peaked nipple and swirl my tongue, a sound escapes Vee's lips, one which wipes the last civilized part of me away.

Roughly, I yank her panties to one side, cock straining as my focus shifts to one thing: being inside Vee. Slipping my hand between her legs, I push a finger inside her and place my lips next to her ear, enjoying the slight hitch in her breath. Her hands slide into my hair, and the hold tightens as I hold my palm against her, moving my fingers and listening to the short, sharp breaths she takes. Her soft hand against my cock drives me further away from any chance I'll be gentle.

I hitch her higher, my length pressing against her soft centre, and her breath rushes out. I hold the tip of myself against her, ready.

Vee drags her mouth away, eyes dark and lips swollen, the pink creeping along her neck to her chest. "Don't stop."

"No chance." She kills me. This woman drives me insane. I don't hold back, can't. I grip Vee's ass and push hard into her. She's tight and hot surrounding my cock, so fucking wet, and I drive into her again and again, seeking the rush and release only Vee can give me.

Her fingers grip my shoulders, nails painful against my skin, and her lips meet mine. I part Vee's legs wider; she could be weightless in my arms, because all I'm aware of is the scent of Vee and sex, the way our skin slides against each other. The space between us disappears in the moment. We're part of each other, the way we both want, and not just physically. I urge her on as she matches my movements with hers, and enjoy how she grips my shoulders tighter, as if she never wants to let go.

The fear something bad will happen disappeared the moment we exploded into this hard, intense, and fucking amazing sex. The last few days have been an eternity, wanting her again.

Vee pushes a hand between us and I move back as she touches herself, chasing her own pleasure too. I watch as her eyes close and teeth graze across her lips. Vee's breaths turn to soft moans as I pick up my urgency. She spurs me on with her movement, murmuring words I can't hear, and she swears and tightens her legs as her body clenches around me. I'm shocked by the rush taking over as I come hard, holding myself inside her as she continues to pulse around me. Vee's legs grip me harder around the waist, harder as she pushes against me, head against the wall as she shudders again.

I cover her face in kisses and she relaxes into my arms, body melting into mine. My heart thumps against hers as I rest my hand against the wall and continue to kiss her.

I never want to lose this girl.

Vee moves to stand and steadies herself against the wall, legs shaking as she looks up at me from beneath her tangled hair. "I told you it wouldn't be the same. Look, I'm still here."

"Yeah. Not the same. Try fucking amazing, Vee." I pull her towards me and hold her face in both hands. "Do you know how much I love you? And that whatever happens, I'm with you. Always."

Vee pushes my damp hair back, "You don't know how much it means to me, to know you love me, and won't reject me now I've changed."

"But you haven't. Something inside may be different, but you're Vee."

"And she still loves you, Ewan." Her words fill my heart until my chest hurts, because I'm surrendering to a part of myself I've denied my whole time here. "This supercharged nuclear Vee," she says and chuckles.

I moisten my lips and trace a finger around her breast to her nipple, and her eyes darken again as it peaks. "Oh, yeah."

We laugh and joke as we dress, and I mean what I said. But I also witnessed Vee do something I could never imagine to the portal, and saw genuine fear in Logan's face when he looked at her. The girl who looked into my eyes as our bodies connected isn't filled with darkness, but with love and affection.

So what has changed?

I am fucking terrified what we might find inside that book.

14

Vee

Ewan pulls into the pub car park on his bike; I sit behind him, clinging on in fear.

Nope. Still not a fan.

As soon as he spotted my nerves, Ewan cut short the ride he was about to take me on, which my trembling body is grateful for. After the powerful sex I just had, I don't need anymore dangerous thrills. Ewan wasn't the only one scared I'd see another vision or fill with pain again. In the back of my mind, I worry what the connection is. With the others, I have Heath's intense light from his magic; Xander's crazy energy breaking things; and Joss's heightened empathy. But Ewan? Is he infecting me with something?

I shake away the thought this could be negative. Not negative, I tell myself. He gave what I needed to take the powers and allow them to grow inside me.

"You okay?" asks Ewan.

There's something about this guy when his hair's messed up and he's wearing his leather jacket. Secret fantasy about rough biker guys covered in tattoos who know how to make a girl scream? I guess that pales against the fantasy I'm living in now. But, hell, this guy just held me against the wall and did wicked things that won't leave my mind right now.

I'm half-disappointed we left the house.

I hand my bike helmet to Ewan. "We weren't as long as Joss thought we would be."

Ewan bites his lip with a smile. "Is that a problem? Not long enough?"

"You know it wasn't." I tug him by the jacket towards me and place my lips on his mouth.

"At least you didn't run screaming this time," he says against my ear and nips the lobe.

Relieved he's dropped some of his intensity, I take his hand and squeeze his fingers. "You know you weren't the reason why."

"Yes," he replies softly and kisses the side of my head. "I know any screaming from now on will be good."

I slap his ass and we walk into the pub, hands still held. The other guys sit at the same table as last time I walked in here, when I was accompanied by Heath instead of Ewan. This time, unlike the last, Xander is here, sitting in the seat I took the first time. My stomach flips at how much has changed in my life despite the surroundings being the same.

Ewan takes his seat beside Joss, and I perch on a spare stool beside him. This time around I don't avoid his touch as he places a hand on my leg. Joss throws us a knowing smile but says nothing.

"Vee, tell me what happened the first time you met these guys. I'm curious." Xander drinks from his bottle.

"I thought I was on a weird date with Heath."

Ewan stares. "You did? A date with the weirdo who stalked you?"

"I did not stalk her," Heath retorts.

"You just happened to lurk outside my house, huh?" I say and poke him affectionately.

Xander glares at Heath. "What? You could've freaked her out. Following Vee was a dumb move."

"Says you, who'd buggered off fuck knows where, without telling us," snaps Heath. "Not exactly helpful."

The conversation stops dead. I need to talk to Heath about the tension he's carrying around—I haven't had a chance since our world shifted planes again.

"Did you know Vee hit Heath with her car?" Joss puts in.

Xander splutters his drink and wipes his mouth. "She deliberately hit you? What did you do to annoy her?"

"Nothing, she's just a bad driver."

I scowl at him. "It was raining and you appeared from nowhere."

"Okay. Fine. I walked in front of your car."

"I knew it!" exclaims Ewan. "I told you, didn't I, Vee?"

I stare at Heath in disbelief. "You did? That was horrible! At first, I thought I'd killed somebody."

"Sorry. We suspected someone else was following you and had to get to you first."

"You could've spoken to me at work. It would've been less painful."

"I tried getting your attention at work and failed. I smiled at you once and after that you never looked at me again. Well, apart from my ass."

I bite down on my lip to prevent a retort as Joss snickers. "She's always staring at your ass, Heath."

"What did *you* think that night I met you all?" I ask Joss, with a glare.

"Wasn't it obvious? I was pretty stunned to finally see you. Almost literally. I could feel your presence before you walked through the door."

"Then why weren't you the one looking for me instead of Heath?" I ask.

Joss lowers his voice. "Because Heath can kill quicker, if needed. Like you saw."

I shift in my seat at the memory. The shocking evening he killed two people, before I realised they were a fae and demon. Two people trying to abduct or kill me. "I remember."

"Anyway, we'd agreed nobody was going to touch you, which I was okay with until I saw you," Joss continues. "Right at that moment I knew you'd be trouble."

"Same," says Ewan.

"I know, you obviously didn't like me when we met," I tell Ewan.

"I was jealous." I blink at his words. "Because you were with Heath and were close to him; I thought he'd gone against our agreement."

"Are you still jealous?" asks Xander with curiosity.

"No. Are you?" retorts Ewan.

"No."

I scratch my cheek. "Do we need a conversation about our relationships? Y'know, sometime after we stop the apocalypse, maybe."

"I think we're all beyond that now, aren't we?" says Joss. "This is a little bit more than four guys in a pub with a girl."

"Yeah, thanks for the reality check, Joss," mutters Heath.

The group lapses into silence and the evening sinks into drinking and the odd joke. I run my finger around my glass's rim. This was supposed to be a night off from stress, but Ewan's checking his phone every five minutes and Xander's constantly scanning the room as if a demon horde might invade at any moment.

The King's Arms was my local, or as much of a local as antisocial Vee had on her nights out with Anna. My stomach twists uncomfortably. I haven't contacted her since I moved into my new world, at first terrified she might not exist, and later I deleted all my contacts around the time I decided not to be human anymore. I could locate her if I wanted, but that world seems distant now.

Anna, who I played pool with in this pub, and whose world I now have to save. *Oh, how life changes.*

"Vee? Are you okay?" I look at a concerned Heath. "You look sad."

"Do you play pool?" I ask.

He grins. "Yeah, and I always win."

"Sure you do, dude," says Ewan.

"Cool. I'll beat you all," I say and stand. Four pairs of eyes regard me with amusement. "What? I will. Who wants to go first?"

"Heath did last time, apparently," Joss says with a sly smile and I smack him lightly across the back of the head. "Or was it Ewan?"

Ewan glowers at him. "Not cool, Joss."

"Bloody hell, I'm joking around!" He huffs. "Sorry if I offended you, Vee."

"I'm amused, not offended." The pool table at the opposite end of the pub is empty with no players around. I indicate the bar. "I'll get the cues."

I head across the pub, honestly amused by Joss's inappropriate comment. Sometimes, he can't help himself and his attempts to lighten situations fail. That could've been one awkward conversation.

The barman, Gary, greets me and I wait for him to remark how long it's been since he saw me. But it hasn't been long. All the crazy shit that's happened recently has been in the space of weeks, when it feels like months.

"Hey, sweetheart."

I turn to the voice on my left as Gary hands me the pool cues. A man with sandy blond hair and drunk eyes, a few years older than me, grins back.

I hate being called sweetheart. Or honey. Or love. In fact, any pet name at all pisses me off. Heath once tried to call me baby, and I told him if he didn't stop I'd slap him. He laughed, until realising I was serious. Did he pass this nugget of information onto the others? Because nobody calls me anything but Vee.

"Hello." I take the cues the barman holds out.

"Do you want a drink?" the guy asks and gestures at the bar.

"No. I have one. I'm with my friends." I indicate the four guys, all in conversation except Xander, who's now looking in my direction.

The man twists his head to look. "Ah. Those four. I've seen them with a few girls in here." He rubs his nose. "You don't look like their usual type."

"I guess their taste changed." I swallow down the rising jealousy from earlier. They've hinted they'd pick up girls in the past; of course they did. Look at them, and I've firsthand experience they know what they're doing in the sex department.

"Yeah. Guess they have." After taking a too-lingering look at my breasts swelling above my black top, he leans in and whispers, "Sometimes girls disappear around here, and I've seen some of them with those guys. Careful you're not the next to disappear."

"I know them well. Thanks for your concern."

He takes his glass of whiskey and drains the contents. "If you need help, just holler."

I give him a tight smile. Early on, this would've worried me, but now I presume the girls were demons. Although I have to be honest with myself and admit some would've been hook-ups.

"Thanks for your concern."

I edge past the man who stinks of cigarettes, gripping the cues, and then back to the table. Xander nods towards the bar. "Who was that?"

"Random guy. Who's playing?" I point at the pool table.

"Hitting on you?" continues Xander, staring back across the pub.

"Don't go alpha on her," says Joss with a sigh. "Vee's an attractive girl, of course guys will hit on her."

"When she walked away, the sleaze watched Vee as if he wanted to eat her alive," Xander snaps.

"Oh, maybe a demon, then?" I ask in a light tone.

"Ha bloody ha." Xander crosses his arms and stares at the guy. I glance over and the man's returning the aggressive look.

"Bloody hell, Xan." Joss pushes his stool back and stands. "Vee."

"Yes?" I look around just as Joss's mouth meets mine. I make a noise of surprise as he rests his lips on mine for a few moments and curls one arm around my waist to hold me closer. Thankfully an affectionate, gentle touch and not full on, because this is directly in front of the other guys.

He withdraws and winks at me. "I guess she's with me, Xander. You gonna stare me down too?"

Xander breaks his gaze at the guy and drinks. "Nope."

I look back at the man, who's turned away. Did Joss's kiss satisfy him I'm taken and not worth hitting on?

"Thanks, Joss," I say. "The last thing we need is you going over the top, Xander."

Xander looks at us impassively. "Yeah. Whatever."

"Any time," says Joss with a laugh. "Hope you didn't mind, Vee."

I shake my head. "All good."

"Food." Ewan interrupts and holds up a menu. "Who's eating?" Xander takes it from him.

"Heath? Playing?" I ask.

"Sure."

I take my cue and head to the pool table. As I place the coloured balls into the triangle, I watch the guys. This situation is ordinary and sharpens into focus how extraordinary they are. A couple of girls who watched us curiously before now seem satisfied I'm with Joss and are attempting to catch the other threes' attention. One of them follows Ewan to the bar when he heads over to order food. Subtle. *Not.* Unsurprisingly, Ewan barely pays her any attention, but I don't miss his aggressive proximity to the guy who hit on me. Oh great, he'd better not be following Xander's example.

Heath approaches and rests against the table then chalks his cue, focusing on the action. A smile plays on his lips as he watches me set up the game.

"You really think you're going to win, don't you?" I ask.

"Yep."

I stand against the nearby wall as Heath takes the first shot, watching as his hair flops into his eyes, and the pursed-lipped concentration. What would've happened if we'd been on a date before he introduced me to the others? Was he ever tempted? For the first time in weeks, I'm reminded of the strange night our lives collided the way my car did with his body.

Recently, Heath's distanced himself and until now, I never noticed. Not deliberately, the way Ewan has, but as if he's further from me since my unknown power increased.

Heath shifts around the table to take a shot in front of me, giving me a great view of the ass that I'm supposedly always staring at. Which of course means I have to again, because why break the habit? His T-shirt rides up, revealing a smooth, muscled lower back.

Hell, I'm a lucky girl.

I'm ashamed to admit that I sometimes thank whoever stuck me in this situation. What if they'd been a bunch of unattractive guys with manners that made Xander look like he could teach etiquette in his spare time?

But then why put us in a situation where I didn't have any desire to "connect" with each and every one of the Horsemen?

Heath misses his latest shot and swears. Straightening, he turns to me and gestures at the table. "Show me what you're made of. I've already potted five."

"Go you," I line up my shot, but can't shake the need to speak to Heath. "How are you coping, Heath?"

"I should ask you that question."

The yellow ball clicks another of mine, spinning it into a pocket. "You're all supporting me, but I've noticed you're quieter than usual."

Heath shrugs. "You know me, 'emo Heath.'"

"Heath..." I warn him; he's well aware that Xander's nickname for him is unfair.

"I'm lost, Vee. That's all. I know we're all struggling to cope, but every time someone new comes on the scene, or

Xander agrees to ally with people we don't trust, I get nervous." He steps forward and traces his finger along the edge of the table. "Mostly I worry about letting you all down."

"How?"

"Take your shot, Vee."

I do as he suggests, but I refuse to leave this. Deftly, I pot most of my balls, smug when I see his surprised expression.

"How so 'let us down'?"

"Not fulfilling my role. Y'know. Not fixing things if they go permanently wrong for one of you." I'm confused by why he's using euphemisms until I notice two guys in ear shot.

"We'll be okay," I say, wishing I was as confident as I sound.

"Maybe, but until we get the stone—"

I interrupt by putting my finger on his lips. "No. We're not talking about that. We're relaxing and playing pool."

Heath pulls his mouth into a rueful smile. "True."

"And I'm winning."

"Huh." He sweeps me closer and bends to place his mouth on mine. "I bet I can distract you."

"I'm sure you can." His hard chest presses against mine and when he kisses me, his longer hair tickles my cheek. Ewan's does too but isn't as long. Heath has more to hold onto—and the thought reminds me how distant we are. "It's been a while since I spent the night with you. I'm sorry I didn't notice you felt alone."

He shakes his head. "I wasn't. Just watching from the sidelines mostly."

"It's not because you're worried about what I am?"

"I hear you say that all the time Vee, and it stabs my heart because there's nothing 'wrong' about you. I mean, if you decided to start tearing your way through British institutions and destroying any demons who are disguised, yeah, then we might worry. But you have yourself under control."

I share his laugh. "Okay. True."

"And you know what, Vee? When this is all over, I'm stepping back. Taking time out. You know how I feel about wanting to be more human. I'm gonna do that."

I chew on a nail as I watch him, hearing the determination in his voice. Ewan says not to worry about the future, but Heath's firmly focused there. "Do you know what I love about what you just said?"

He takes the cue, readying himself to continue. "That I don't think you're hellbent on killing?"

"No. That you said 'when this is all over'. That you believe this will end well."

Heath pushes hair from his face, bright green eyes shining as he studies me. "I meant Chaos. Once he's gone, the world will change, one way or the other."

"But *we* won't," I whisper. "We'll always be us."

Heath chalks his cue and nods. "I hope so."

I close my eyes and drag myself away from his seriousness. The click of pocketed balls brings me back to the game and I'm shocked to see Heath's almost won.

Edging closer, I wait until he's about to take the shot and slide my hand across his ass before pushing my hand into his pocket. Missing the shot, Heath snaps his head around. "Vee... that's cheating!"

I smirk. "And I can always distract you."

15

EWAN

I'm terrified to look away from the online world for more than five minutes, even if we're supposed to be switching off for a few hours. How's that bloody possible? Maybe the others can fool themselves things aren't as bad as they appear, but I've come face to face with Seth in his true form.

This...*thing* is pure evil. I've met a crap load of creatures who do shit I never want to think about again, but I've no doubt that Seth is capable of more. And I'm sure he wants to show us that.

The little pantomime with me, Vee, and Joss by the portal was him flexing his muscles. Showing us his power. Can he drag Vee to him any time he wants? If he does that before we figure out who she is and why, things could end badly and quickly.

We have one last card in our hands, and it's not Vee. We

have the book, and the answers soon. He doesn't have all the facts and can't carry out his destructive plans until he does. Heath's confused and asked if Seth's a god with his power and the capacity to destroy everything, why hasn't he?

Isn't the answer obvious?

He's violent. Sadistic. We've only seen three deaths he's responsible for, but how many more will we witness? Chaos wants to have fun and watch human life suffer at his hands. He told us as much—they're insects crawling across the world he created. The world he wants destroyed.

Personally, I'd like to track him down and rip him to pieces, but even Xander knows this is futile without all the facts. We could die. All of us.

No. Once we're in full possession of the knowledge held in this cryptic book, we attack first. We follow to the letter what it says to do.

But even then, we'd need to find him first.

I fidget, checking the phone again. Vee finished her pool game with a sulky Heath and now sits between him and me as Joss and Xander play. Does this protect Vee from teleporting? It never did with me and Joss, but at least if Seth pulls a stunt like that again, they'll both go with her.

I take a drink then swipe my mouth before combing the internet on my phone: message boards, breaking news, anything with a hint what Seth could be doing.

I don't need to.

Because, of course, the bastard prefers to taunt.

<I told you a storm was coming>

A message from Seth, with a link. Early reports from a weather station. A huge hurricane has formed in the Atlantic, sudden and not predicted by long-range weather forecasts.

"Shit." I scroll through the site, the calculations for when the storm will reach landfall as a category 5. The hurricane is headed straight for areas with dense population, and with it, worries there'll be greater devastation than Hurricane Katrina. Lives will be lost and homes destroyed. "Heath, get Joss and Xander. Now."

Heath calls them over, and Xander holds his hand out for my phone. "What's happening, Ewan?"

I run through options in my head as Xander reads, stony-faced, before passing to Heath. My phone sounds and Heath blinks rapidly as he reads the message.

<Two days until landfall. Bring me the book.>

"Fucking arsehole," I growl.

Xander's face pinches, and he strategises in his head as I do. "Do you think he has the other part of the stone?"

"No."

I wave a hand. "We have to consider he might. We won't know until Syv and the Collector return."

"I'll call her. We focus on Seth." Xander stands and pulls out his phone. He wanders to a quieter corner, but not before draining his beer first.

"Do we reply?" I ask.

The phone beeps again.

<Come on, boys. Aren't you supposed to save the world? I want to see all of you. Bring Vee.>

I stand too. "We need to leave. Now."

The situation cuts short our night out, but how could this have ended any other way? The decision is made not to interact with Seth until we get home. Negotiating with him over a beer in the pub isn't a good idea.

I'm home first, and a good few minutes before everyone else. Vee knows the trip on my bike will be a fast and unpleasant one, so travels with the others instead.

They finally arrive as I pace around the lounge clutching the phone in one hand, watching for a message like a hawk watching prey.

"Anything else from Seth?" asks Xander as he drops his jacket over the sofa.

"No. He must be waiting for a response. Probably smirking to himself that he's scared us into silence."

Heath sinks back on the sofa and drags both hands down his face. "Why a storm? I expected him to go after us or attack a portal again. Why this?"

Joss perches on the sofa arm. "He's digging at our weakness, isn't he? Humans."

"But we can't stop the weather," puts in Heath. "This is impossible."

"Yeah, but Seth can—he created it. We stop *him*." Xander jabs a finger at the phone.

"How? By giving him what he wants?" asks Joss. "Taking Vee and the book to him?"

"Be serious," sneers Xander. "No."

"We need to know where he is, though," Heath says. "Reply and ask where."

I do and there's no response for a few moments, until a picture message comes through. Seth. Grinning. Sitting in a desert, surrounded by green scrub and a huge blue sky above the barren land stretching into the shimmering horizon behind him.

<Wish you were here xx>

In his sick selfie, bodies on the sand surround him in a circle, like a gruesome protection rune.

"What the fuck?" I breathe. "Are they human?"

Xander grabs the phone and places his fingers on the screen to zoom in. "I can't tell. I doubt it."

"Screw this." I swipe to open the video calling app, ignoring Xander's words not to bother because Seth won't answer.

They always underestimate him, and that's partly how we're in this fucking mess.

Of course the bastard can't resist the opportunity.

"Hey, boys!" Seth's face appears onscreen. "How was your evening?"

"Where are you?" asks Xander.

Seth pulls the phone away from his face and he sweeps it around him. "Do you have names for your portals? Like Disneyland does? Is this one Fae World? I'm still hoping one of the six is Dragon World."

I inhale and concentrate on not retorting. What is it about him and fucking dragons?

Joss turns to a pale-faced Vee. "Has he attacked a portal?"

"I don't know." Her response is barely a whisper.

"I can't sense anything has touched one," puts in Heath. "We usually do."

"Fucking mind tricks," mutters Xander, then says to Seth, "Tell us where you are, and we'll tell you which portal you're near." I look at Xander in horror. We can't give him anymore information, is he insane?

Seth pans the phone to the neatly arranged bodies, lying with heads touching feet, bodies curved into a macabre modern art display. "Which portal did you send these idiots to protect? And why the hell are others doing your job?"

"Holy shit," mutters Heath. "There're ten bodies there."

"I always thought fae had the prettiest eyes." Seth zooms in on a victim's face. Then another. Where each victim's eyes once were, there are two black scorch marks in a bloodied, mask-like face .

"Where were the fae sent to protect a portal?" I mutter at Heath.

"The States," he whispers back.

"Shit."

Xander turns away, as he does when trying to hide how he feels, and Vee watches, sitting forward as if about to go to him.

My horror vies with anger—and panic. "Have you opened the portal?"

Seth returns the camera to his gleeful face and snickers. "I think you'd know if I had. Don't you? You can hide one demon dog, but if a whole tribe of fuck-knows-what's behind this portal escape, I'm sure the humans might *just* notice."

I breathe out relief. That's one thing, and proof he's killing time.

"Maybe Seth can't open them," Heath says quietly. "Maybe he needs the book to work out how."

"He did something to the last portal though," says Joss. "He can definitely open them if he wants."

"Maybe he needs Vee there?" Heath glances at her. Vee now stands with Xander, hand on his arm as they speak in low voices.

"You think he needs Vee to open them? Is that what's in the book?" I whisper.

"Hello? Guys? Pay attention!" calls Seth. "I had this idea I wanted to run by you."

My stomach flips over as he moves one of the bodies into a position he can lean himself against. Sharpened fae features. Young. Hair the colour of Logan's. These must be the newly created powerful fae he arranged to guard portals. To help us.

And they died.

Seth holds the phone above his head and looks up. "I think the world needs to know what lives amongst them." He lifts and drops the arm of the dead body. "Hey! Should I drop these guys off in the middle of a city? I bet people would love to see what real fae look like. That would be cool!"

I stare at his insane babbling. Cool?

"Do what you want with them," replies Xander in a cold tone. "We never guaranteed their safety. Portia and Logan can deal with this issue."

"Xander." He jerks as Heath pushes him. "Don't be fucking stupid."

"Does that mean Portia will want to catch up with me too? Awesome. Hey, do you think I can still go see her theatre performance? When is it? I could hold off my plans until she's had her chance to shine. I really did like her." Seth shields his eyes and the phone against the brightness. Okay. Now I can't tell if he's genuinely taking the piss, or just mad.

Xander snorts. "I doubt the fae will send someone so important to risk death by meeting you."

Seth's face moves closer to the camera and his voice cools. "But the Horsemen will bring *their* most important when they meet me. Where is she?"

Vee steps beside me and into view. "Here. Planning how to kill you." Her voice could cut diamonds, sharp and precise.

Seth's laughter peals around. "You still think that's why you're here? To kill me? That's cute."

"So you know who I am?" she asks.

He pulls a face and shrugs. "Yeah and nah. I'm missing the crucial information, like you guys are. Hence. Bring. Me. The. Book."

Xander laughs at him. "Pointless if you can't translate it."

"But I'll have the ability soon. I know you have part of the stone needed to decipher the book, and I hope you'll see sense and give it to me." He pauses. "And Vee? That was really not nice killing my friend. He was helping me."

"He was going to kill Syv," she growls.

"Oh, her. Clever girl finding what I need to decipher the book. You know, the book you're going to bring to me so I don't rain on everybody's parade." Seth smirks at his stupid joke. "Shame she gave it to the wrong people, but she won't find the other half. I have someone else following her. You don't think a half-demon chick and her fairy boyfriend can stop me taking the other half of the stone, do you?"

I swallow. What situation have we sent Syv and the Collector into?

"Are you expecting us to come to you there?" asks Xander. "Because that's not going to happen."

"How many people do you think would die if the hurricane hit?" asks Seth.

"How many people will die if you translate the book?" Xander shoots back.

Seth places a hand on his chest. "Alexander," he gasps. "Are you back to justifying collateral damage again?"

"What the fuck does that mean?"

"You'll find out." He throws a smile. "But anyway, do what I ask, and I'll save some lives. If not, you'll be responsible for painful deaths. You know it's the disease that comes after the destruction which kills most of them, and you can't stop that. When I end this world and kill them all, it will be quick at least. It never takes insects long to die if you squash them quick." He pokes a body next to him. "It took the fae a while to die, though."

I rub my eyes. There's no right answer here; people will die.

Xander grabs the phone from me and disconnects the call. "Xander!" I protest.

"I'm not getting involved in his games. We have two days. Syv will be back with the stone, and we'll have the upper hand."

"So we wait and hope he doesn't fuck something up in the mean time?" Heath retorts.

"What else do you suggest?" Xander snaps. "That we go to him?"

I screw my face up as a Xander and Heath argument kicks off.

Heath steps forward, into Xander's face. "Chaos could open the portal he's near."

"That's a risk I'm willing to take."

"And the storm?"

"That's not going to happen."

"Really? How can you be so sure?"

Vee reaches out and pulls Xander's hand from his pocket; she tightens her fingers around his. "Guys. Seth's not in the same room as us, and he's still causing divisions."

Heath huffs and steps back. "Vee's right. We'll need a united front when we talk to Portia."

"Portia?" asks Xander, eyes widening. "Oh, no. No fucking way. Logan can deal."

Heath takes a deep breath. "Didn't you just see? How many fae were slaughtered trying to help us and the world against Chaos? Why do you think he chose that location and not one of the portals guarded by Ripley's forces?"

I blink at him and Joss interjects, "Because he knows the

Order and Logan are allied with us right now, but that Portia isn't fully aware of Logan's actions. He also knows how little Portia trusts any of us. She'll lose her shit when she finds fae were used in this way, all behind her back."

"Exactly," says Heath. "If Portia spits the dummy and refuses to help anymore, then he's eliminated one of his allied enemies without having to lift another finger."

"Possibly two," says Joss quietly. "Fuck knows what Portia will do to Logan when she discovers the whole truth."

They're right.

Chaos has one strategy he can always use. One used before with huge effect.

Divide and conquer.

16

Vee

The next morning, I wander around the house fighting anxiety after last night's switch from relaxing to shocking. After all the recent stress and horror, I would've thought some quiet alone time would be good, but I don't want to spend time in my current headspace.

Especially when images of myself in the mirror at the museum sneak in alongside the gruesome fae images. Is that how I look when I kill now? Or something more sinister?

But like Xander, I want to act and not think too hard. The urge to fight for an answer—and confront anything that gets in my way—won't leave. I have another fight: to keep the other Vee under control; the one who wants to walk out the house and find Seth. That's harder after seeing the result of his attack last night.

I head to see Joss. I'm concerned about our conversation

at the museum; perhaps talking to him about how we both feel right now would help. We haven't spoken much about recent events. Is he coping? Or hiding from me, the way Ewan did, after what happened in Scotland?

I can't allow myself to think about Seth and his threats. The idea sickens and terrifies me.

I can relax with Joss the most and right now I need his gentle calm. I head upstairs and find Joss in his room on the bed, reading. He's barefoot and wearing just a T-shirt with his jeans. I only see the guys wrapped up against winter in their jackets when we're out, and I appreciate how the grey material stretches tight across his shoulders, and his muscled arms emerging from the sleeves. Involuntarily, I picture his long fingers stroking my skin and not in the soothing way I've approached him for.

"Stop perving, Vee." Joss's eyes remain on his book, but a smile hovers around his lips.

"I was not," I protest and head toward the bed.

"Uh huh." He lowers the book.

Sitting, I tip my head to read the book's title. The Da Vinci Code. "Joss! That's fiction, and won't help your obsession with religion."

He pulls a face and sets the book on the nightstand. "I feel like a fiction break."

"Hmm."

"But now I have you to spend time with."

Smiling, I stretch out on the bed and prop myself up on my elbows, so I face Joss, and place my feet in his lap.

Joss tuts. "Oh, I see. You only came to see me for a foot massage." He mock pouts.

"No. But if you insist..."

He shakes his head before taking my foot and kneading with strong fingers. "I sense you're not okay."

"What? You sense that from my feet?" I joke.

"Ha ha. No. Come on, speak to me."

"I can't cope," I whisper. "I can't stop worrying about you all and how you're being affected by this."

He looks up. "A lot is happening, of course, you worry."

'A lot is happening'. I almost laugh at his understatement. "True."

"Let's make a deal. For a couple of hours, we relax. There's nothing we can do right now until we meet with Ripley and the others and discuss what to do."

"I need you to know what happened to me doesn't change anything between us all," I blurt out.

"But it does." My heart speeds in fear over what he might say. "Don't you feel like this has broken some of the tension? Built trust? Maybe because Seth has gone, maybe because Ewan somehow united us. I don't know."

Relief replaces the concern. "I think so."

"And when this shit is over, then we can spend more time together. I don't think anybody is going to blame you for being a little distant. You're stressed. We all are."

"So I need some of the Joss treatment to wipe away stress." I grin at him, but he doesn't return my smile.

"Believe me, Vee, you don't want some Joss treatment right now."

I wriggle my toes. "Why?" He looks up, and my heart speeds at the look in his eyes. Desire. Unhidden, pure desire. Am I in another situation like Ewan last night?

"Maybe I do."

"Don't, Vee," he whispers. He eyes the open door and shifts to massage my ankle. "You think I'm obsessed with thoughts of Hell and God? Believe me, that's nothing compared to the obsession I have with you right now."

My heart speeds, his touch sending not-so-soothing

sensations through me. I came up here to relax and joke; this intensity is unusual from Joss. He slides a hand higher, massaging my calf as he looks back at me.

I pull my leg away and move, so I'm beside him instead, wanting the comfort we're agreeing to share.

He reaches out and touches my face. "I know you come to me when you want peace and gentle treatment." I open my mouth to protest. "Vee, you know that's true. The problem is, I don't feel very gentle right now."

His eyes burn with an intensity that snatches my breath. I've seen this from Joss once when we were in the study that night, and for a few blissful moments, I saw the raw man underneath. But he's right, and so was Syv when she spoke about how intuitive he is. This man puts my needs first, always, sometimes frustratingly so, as if he's scared what would happen if he doesn't hold back.

"You're worried you'll lose control around me, is that what you mean?"

He leans forward and brushes his lips on mine, sending sparks across my scalp. "No. I would be very in control, Vee."

His words murmured against my mouth, trigger heat, instantly, spreading through my body as it instantly responds to the suggestion. "Why's that a bad thing?"

He smoothes my hair. "I don't want to scare you."

I can't help but break into a laugh. "Joss, there's more to scare me in my life than you suggesting you want to do bad things to me."

His grip tightens. "I want to be alone with you. To take you somewhere away from all this and—"

"And?"

"Seriously, I'm not going to say anything that's in my head right now because just you with me, like this, is driving me towards showing you instead."

"Close the door, then," I whisper.

"No. Not today. Not in the middle of all this. I want you to myself, just for a few hours, away from the other guys. Maybe that's selfish, but it's true. I don't mean that I'm jealous because I know how we all have something different to give you. It's just..." He sighs. "I'm not explaining myself well, am I?"

I place my finger on his lips. "I understand. How about just a kiss?"

I hardly get the words out before Joss's mouth crashes on mine, wiping the confusion over the whole situation away. The suddenness matches my surprising, overwhelming need to respond. I grab Joss round the neck and kiss him back. Hard. He grips my hair in his fist, holding my head so I can't move, deepening his kiss. His resolve is snatched away; I can tell by the intensity of the moment, and I relish the way his tongue explores my mouth, sharing the intoxication.

Joss holds my waist with his other arm and pulls me onto his lap. I dig my fingers into his shoulders, and the kiss continues; neither of us stopping for air.

His hands roam to my backside, and he shifts below me. When I dive my hands beneath his T-shirt and drag my nails across his abs, Joss pulls his mouth away. Our hot, heavy breaths mingle as he rests his forehead on mine.

"Just a kiss isn't possible, Vee. You have no fucking idea what you do to me."

I shuffle from side to side on top of him. "I can feel what I do to you, Joss. I know you want to fuck me."

He groans and pushes me back onto the bed, nudging my legs apart with his knee. "Shush! Don't say things like that." He studies me, eyes darkened by the need to let go. "Seriously, my self-control is crap right now."

"Well, maybe it's a good thing the bedroom door is open." I chew my lip and wait for his response.

Joss takes a ragged breath. "If you let me close the bedroom door, I won't be responsible for my actions."

I push him away from me. "Close the door, Joss."

17

Vee

Since the stakes shifted in the world, we haven't had the misfortune of an audience with Portia. She's refused to meet us or Ripley, and she moved herself and family to the fae court in London. There, the more powerful wards provide greater protection than her suburban home and security guards. I'm surprised she agreed to co-operate at all, and it sounds like Logan hasn't been one hundred percent honest with her. I won't be surprised if today ends that co-operation.

Especially following Ewan's chat with Logan about the bodies in the desert. Logan has no choice but to tell Portia everything now, because she didn't know they were there. These were his 'troops'.

The morning after Seth's communication, our urgency increases. Xander receives news from Syv that her and the Collector are safe and will hopefully locate the stone today.

We're all on edge over what might happen. Although the Collector could probably defend himself against Seth or anybody he sends after them, we don't know if he's anywhere near as powerful as we are.

Xander also receives an excruciating phone call from Portia, which we can hear from across the kitchen. He repeatedly tells her to calm down and 'we need to meet and talk about this' before giving up and holding the phone away from his ear. He pulls a face at us and rolls his eyes. I can't help laughing at the scene, as if he's a husband who can't stand listening to an earful from his wife.

Eventually she quiets and Xander wanders from the room to the next, resuming the conversation.

"He's doing well," I say to the other guys.

Ewan looks over from where he's organising weapons on the table, lining up and inspecting daggers—and guns, which is something I don't often see. "You mean he's being polite to the woman he doesn't like?"

"No, I mean with keeping hold of the War who negotiates and strategises rather than storms in or tries to push his opinion on people."

"I think he knows that won't work in this situation," says Heath. "But I agree, this isn't like my brother at all."

Joss, sitting besides Ewan, picks up a gun and examines it. "I'm not looking forward to the next little get-together with our new *friends*."

"I suggest you leave that behind!" I point at the gun.

Joss laughs. "Of course."

"As long as Xander persuades her to meet the Order too," says Ewan.

"Did Logan manage to convince her that Chaos was behind the assassination attempt and not the Order?" asks Heath.

Ewan snorts. "I think that will probably be the last thing on the agenda, after they have a 'nice chat' about how Logan went behind her back and created an army of powerful fae. If I were her, I'd have him locked away—or dead."

Heath chuckles. "Well, has anybody heard from him since Scotland?"

Xander wanders back into the room and tosses his phone on the table, hair messed from repeatedly rubbing his hand across his head.

"Logan had the balls to talk to her first. She's pissed off and doesn't want to be involved anymore."

"What?" asks Heath incredulously.

"But... I've persuaded her to meet with us all. Maybe between us we can convince her to help."

"All? Ripley too?"

"Yes. Apparently she has news for us."

"Uh oh."

"More theatrics, I'll bet," mutters Ewan. "She doesn't give a shit about half her subjects. I bet she's using this as an excuse to duck out of the dirty work."

"Maybe, but at least if we all sit down together we may persuade her otherwise."

"Any more word from Seth, Ewan?"

He shakes his head. "We've little time until that storm hits. I hope Syv gets back soon. And in one piece."

"I'm sure she will," Joss replies.

I trace a pattern on the table with my finger. I'm not as confident but keep the thoughts to myself.

XANDER

Portia and Ripley debated over where the meeting should be held, and Ripley backed down to meet where Portia wanted. Our get-together is arranged for the same afternoon, at one of the larger, fae-owned law firms in the City. Walking through the bright and airy offices, it was easier to spot humans and fae based on their reaction to us. The fae watched with suspicion, the humans with interest. Four casually dressed guys each showing the strain of recent days, and Vee in jeans marched through. I bet they think we're dodgy clients.

Logan already waits with a second man, in a scene reminiscent of our meeting at Alasdair's house. I don't recognise him until he speaks. However, and whoever, he hides himself as, Ripley's voice is always recognisable. I'm amused he's chosen a younger model this time, as if he's attempting to fit our look. Perhaps posing as a good looking twenty-something guy helps Ripley persuade people to do what he wants—or allows him to steal their gym-fit bodies? As his dark brown eyes meet mine, and his cheeks dimple into a smile, I shudder to think what's happened to the man he's claimed this time.

Ewan seems to catch my thoughts. "What happened to Alasdair?"

Ripley blows air into his cheeks. "I told you, I was only borrowing him. Alasdair's fine; he'll be released from hospital soon. Poor guy, quite delirious. Anyone would think he'd taken some of the drugs he fights against."

I close my eyes. Great.

"You'd better not be killing people," I snap, "or this arrangement is off."

Ripley tips his chair back and places his boots on the table, hands behind his head and elbows at right angles. "No. I'm hurt that you asked me the question. I told you—ceasefire. Let me ask you the same: have you killed demons?"

"No."

I bite down on my lip. Does the one working for Seth count?

"Then our truce stands."

I scowl and look to Logan. "How're things in the fae world?"

He narrows his eyes at my snide comment. "There's some friction."

Ewan coughs a laugh. "I'll bet."

"Where's Breanna?" asks Heath, looking around.

"We don't know," says Ripley. I tense. With Seth? Do we trust her? "Like the Collector, she's her own person. She will be researching, I imagine."

"Researching what? We need the help she offered."

Ripley shrugs and pulls a face. "Who cares, as long as whatever she's doing also helps us."

"Do you trust her?" asks Joss.

"As much as I trust you." Ripley looks down his nose at Joss.

Mutual feeling, mate. After the weeks with Seth, I don't trust anyone new, including Breanna.

The door opens, and Portia walks into the law firm's conference room, flanked by two bodyguards. She's dressed immaculately in a short black coat and hair swept up as if she's a blonde Audrey Hepburn. Her red-painted mouth thins as she undoes buttons, eyes fixed on the group. They land on the demon.

"I presume you're Ripley?" She half-spits his name as she hands her coat to the tall man on her left.

Ripley stands and gives a small bow. He'd better not be taking the piss or things will descend pretty quickly.

Portia's mouth curls further, as if he's a fly needing to be squashed, and looks to her fae colleague instead. "Logan."

"Portia," he replies evenly.

"Have you begun fixing that little *problem* you created?" she asks, voice terse. They stare at each other and Logan doesn't respond. "Because your betrayal is on the edge of unforgivable." A violet energy crackles faintly and I glance at the glass-panelled walls. Are any employees sneaking a look in?

One thing with fae, if they want to hide how they feel, they can. Is it possible to hide from each other too? Logan doesn't show any fear of the woman who could order his death, which worries me. How powerful has he become with his new followers?

"This isn't the place to talk, Portia. You were quite clear earlier," he replies.

"I've had time to think since then."

"Do you think the fairies are going to kill each other?" whispers Ripley with a smile. "That won't help matters, enough already died yesterday."

"And taunting won't help either!" hisses Ewan. "You're bloody lucky Seth didn't wipe out your colleagues at the other portals."

Fortunately, Portia's focus on Logan prevents her hearing Ripley's jibe.

The second bodyguard pulls out a chair for Portia to sit, and she smooths her black skirt as she does. "I'm not staying long. I have no more interest in your crusade. I'm out."

I nod at Heath. "Told you."

"Don't you think that's a little difficult, Portia, since you live in the world a god could destroy?" puts in Ripley.

Portia gives a serene smile and folds her hands on the table in front of her. "Oh, but we're not staying in this world."

The room drops into a confused silence. "Where are you going?" asks Joss.

"Back to my own realm."

Portia has said some stupid, selfish and insane things before, but *this*? "How, exactly?" I ask.

She wrinkles her nose as if we're asking a dumb question. "Through the portal where my race originally entered."

"How?" repeats Heath.

I thought Seth was mad, but this is insane.

She waves a hand at Logan. "You and your 'new' fae can take over. You were going to overthrow me anyway." He opens his mouth to protest and she holds up a hand to silence him. "Don't patronise me by denying this, you stupid man."

"Bye then!" Ripley waves a hand then folds his arms, amusement lighting his face. "Nice to finally meet you before you left."

"No. Wait." Logan sits forward. "Why would you go back to the wasteland that place has become?"

Portia sniffs. "Why would you stay in the middle of an apocalypse?"

"And you have no power over there!" He shakes his head. "Your family were hated. You'd never survive, even if the climate didn't kill you."

"My life has been threatened, repeatedly, recently. My

ancestors left the fae realm because they feared for their lives. Now I fear for mine and my family's, and I would rather take a risk against the corrupt fae living there, than stay here."

"Are you taking Elyssia?" Vee asks incredulously. "Does she know?"

"I think you're all missing the point," says Heath. "We can't let Portia open a portal and let through the fae her family ran from. I don't know what she means by 'corrupt', but I'm guessing that's not a good thing."

Portia's mouth twitches. "Logan and his betraying bastards can take them out easily. The fae over there don't contain strong magic to bring with them."

Logan shakes his head. "This is a moot point. Portia can't open the portal. She doesn't have the means."

"And the Horsemen will stop her," I growl.

"I don't have the means *yet*. But somebody I know does."

I shake my head. Seth's decision to divide us has bigger consequences than even he could dream of. I always worried Ripley would want to open his portal and let through demon hordes, but I never imagined anybody would leave.

I drag a hand through my hair and stand. We can't deal with all this. "Not happening, Portia."

She stands too. "Yes. It is. Between you all, you have killed too many of my people. I will offer them a choice."

We're interrupted by a light rap on the door, and Logan calls for the person to come in. A young woman in a business suit fails to hide her curiosity as she gestures behind her.

"There are two more people here to join the meeting. I wasn't sure if you were expecting them."

Vee

Syv pushes past the girl and walks into the room. She's never the model of elegance, but I don't think the distressed look to her clothes is deliberate. Her jacket sleeve is torn and her red hair pulled into a pony tail out of her face. Under my scrutiny, she self-consciously touches her injured cheek with a hand covered in scratches. As she moves them, her jacket slips up and I can see deep slashes on her forearms.

Is she injured? Was this Seth?

She sits and places her dirty boots on the chair beside her, crossed at the ankles.

I smile, even though her appearance worries me. That's Syv. Always makes an entrance.

"Are you okay?" asks Joss as he stands.

"Paris is nice this time of year." She forces a smile. "Locals weren't too friendly though. You know how it is."

I look to Joss, who nods in understanding before sitting next to Syv. "Are you sure you're okay?"

Syv jerks her arm away where he places his fingers on her. "Hands off."

With a sigh, Joss shifts to one side but hopefully his proximity will soothe her.

What the hell happened?

The Collector steps in too, bringing with him the strange, imposing presence the tall guy does. Considering the Horsemen's usual dominating personalities, that's quite a feat. His pale skin is untouched, and now that I see him with other fae I see why he avoids human company so much. His eyes are more violet, face longer with a more Elven look to his features. Are fae where stories about elves come from? Despite his captivating looks, there's a harsher expression, especially when he lays eyes on Portia.

The tension between them doesn't need mine and Joss's skills to detect; the suspicion and downright hatred are tangible. I wait for them to acknowledge each other but they don't speak before a focused Xander interrupts.

"Did you see Seth? Did you find the stone?"

I frown at him and he looks surprised that I'm annoyed by his bluntness.

"I'd be in a body bag if Col hadn't been with me," Syv says with a snort. "I have your stone. You'd better pay me a truckload for this, because I'm not joking about the risk to my life."

The Collector moves to the edge of the room and leans against the wall, arms crossed as he watches the assembled allies. "We encountered some issues and Syv was fortunate I was there."

I look at Syv's hands, which tremble; when she sees me looking, she sits on them and scowls.

"Issues?" asks Logan.

"Seth has some interesting tools at his disposal." The Collector's voice holds the calm tone I noticed in the past.

Heath leans closer, elbows on the table. "What tools? Should we be worried?"

"Not about this particular 'tool', no. I've dealt with it," he replies. Syv glances at him and bites her lip but doesn't elaborate. "All that matters is you have your stone. We're here to deliver it, and then I need to rest."

"Not before we've spoken," puts in Portia.

The Collector slowly turns his eyes to hers, and the

disdain in them eclipses any I've seen on Portia's face in the past.

"About?" he asks in a flat tone.

Ripley shifts his feet from the chair and leans forward with glee. "Apparently Portia's headed back to her broken fae realm."

The Collector makes a derisive noise. "How are you going to do that?"

She narrows her eyes. "You know how."

"I do?"

His feigned innocence worries me but Portia snaps, "You know damn well. You have the means."

"But not the inclination."

"You're a disgrace to your race," she sneers. "Worse than this one who's stabbed me in the back." Logan straightens as she points at him. "Our realm will be more intact than this world will be in a few days. I'm willing to take my chances; I have enough fae who'll accompany me, I'm sure. We can start our society again."

The Collector's brows tug closer in amusement at her outburst. "You have little faith in your allies here."

"Correct." Portia stands and takes her coat from her security guard. "I have come to tell you all my position, and I intend to carry out this plan, with or without your agreement."

Just when I thought things couldn't get any worse.

She addresses the Collector. "Perhaps you need to reconsider your options. The writing is on the wall. Your realm needs you again."

"There is a reason I left. I want nothing to do with the place."

As she shrugs the coat back on, her lips thin and she gives the Collector a filthy look. "I hope you regain some sense, and realise where your loyalties lie after hundreds of years hiding from your responsibilities. You're a disgrace to your race! Why anybody ever revered you, I will never know."

"Be careful," he growls.

She brushes her skirt into place. "Fine. We only want you to open the way through; you don't need to come with us. Do it."

He regards her in silence and the guys exchange looks. What's happening here?

In typical Portia style, she stalks from the room, calling back to the Collector that she'll be in touch.

"You can open the portal?" Xander asks incredulously as the door closes. "You better fucking hadn't."

"I would like to see what secrets the books hold first," he replies.

His words are implied: *and then he'll make his decision, despite what he said to Portia.*

Ripley slaps his hands on the table. "Well, this meeting suddenly became more entertaining than expected!"

Xander slumps back in his chair and nods at the Collector. "Who has the stone? Syv or you?"

Syv delves into her pockets and pulls out a roughly hewn grey stone, one that looks as if it matches the part we found in Cambridge.

Joss reaches out to take the stone and turns it over in his hands. "I don't understand how this will help; these look like exactly the same symbols as the other half."

"That's where Breanna can help," says Ripley. "Hopefully she'll be back soon."

"Hopefully?" coughs Ewan. "She better bloody had be."

"I'm sure she wants to save the world too," replies Logan.

I look over as the fae breaks his silence. What does he

think about Portia offering to hand him her kingdom on a plate? Or is he also considering leaving?

Xander pulls the other stone from his pocket; he hasn't let it out of sight since Syv gave him it. Taking the new one from Joss, he places them close. A collective breath is held, replaced by relieved smiles when the pair fit together and match.

"We're taking this with us, until Breanna returns." Xander stands and snatches the stones from the table.

"Why you?" retorts Ripley.

"Because this concerns us! I don't trust you."

"And what if I don't trust you?" he asks and stands too.

Ewan sits forward. "Tough. The Collector has the book, and we have the stones. Don't worry, we'll keep you informed what this says. When Breanna returns she can check over our findings."

Ripley curls his lip at Xander, who interrupts his response. "Don't you think interpreting this sooner rather than later will help us all? Yes, all this goes against everything I believe in but—"

"You're in a vulnerable position?" suggests Logan.

Xander throws him a scowl. "We're leaving. Now. We need to figure this out as soon as possible. Contact Breanna."

The Collector steps forward. "I can help, because I think you'll struggle to do this alone. I have more practice with this kind of thing."

Xander smiles and waves a hand at him. "There you go. A neutral third party."

"Sure he is." Ripley stands. "You agree to see Breanna as soon as she returns."

"We want to see her," I say. "Because until we do, I'm sure we won't find all the answers."

Syv stretches out her shoulders. "Are we headed back,

Col? I need to grab my gear from your place, and then I'm heading out for a drink. Several drinks."

The Collector nods. "Yes. Horsemen, I would like you to bring the stones to me and we can attempt to translate the text together. If you have any other books that could help, please collect them and come to my house."

As Xander pushes the stones into his pocket, Ripley ends his protest, aware he's beaten.

18

Joss

Something's wrong.

As Heath drives closer to the farmhouse, I sense the wards are broken, or at least damaged in some way. Vee sits besides me and leans forward to survey the driveway.

"Do you feel that, Joss?" she whispers and looks to me.

"I haven't felt something like this since the day in the car park, when Ewan was attacked."

"Shit." Heath pulls the car to one side and stops horizontally across the driveway to prevent Xander's car passing. Immediately, Xander slams his brakes on and jumps from the car. I lower my window as he approaches.

"What the fuck, dude?" He throws his hands upwards.

Vee leans around me. "Something's here."

Xander steps back and sweeps a gaze around. "Seth?"

"We can't detect Seth," I reply. "No. Something I can't identify."

"Shit! What? Do we leave? How bad is it?"

I climb from the car and scratch an eyebrow as I look around. "I'm not sure. Strong enough that we can feel it from here."

All five of us are out of the cars and together, Xander's hand in his pocket, clenched around the stone. We stand slightly apart, turning to survey the flat landscape surrounding the fields, gazing into the trees.

The world remains still.

My heart beats faster and the power inside grows, triggered harder by whatever waits for us.

"I can't figure exactly where either. The whole estate reeks of something weird. Whatever this is may not be in the house. Should we check everywhere?"

"We should've expected this," says Heath in a low voice. "Seth broke the wards once before, when he left the fae body and his bloodied message."

Ewan huffs. "Oh yeah, and when he fucking lived with us."

Vee looks at the ground, hair hanging forward and obscuring her face. I poke Ewan and nod at her.

"Do you think this is what they saw in Paris? Is this something still looking for the stone?" I interrupt.

"No, the Collector said he'd dealt with that."

"Stop hanging around talking. Come on. Who's going inside the house, and who's checking the other buildings?" asks Ewan.

"I'll take Vee to see what she can sense; Heath, you can go in with Joss. Ewan, wait outside." Xander pulls out the stones. "I'll keep hold of these."

"No, don't keep them together. Give one to somebody else—Vee's the strongest."

I look to Heath. None of us have spoken the words before, but he's right, whether Xander likes it or not. With a curt nod, he starts walking to the edge of the fields and towards the old barn. Hesitantly, I open the door to the house. Vee follows Xander.

Vee

Xander hands the stone to me. "Heath's right. We don't want one person holding them both if we do meet something." We continue to tramp toward the barn. "Can you sense anything around here?"

I close my eyes and inhale, the earthy winter scent muddled by the acrid smell assaulting me when demons are around.

"It's fainter here."

"So we're headed the wrong way?" he asks.

"I definitely felt the presence stronger near the house."

"Let's take a quick look here anyway." I nod and follow as he stomps away again. "The barn. Maybe the *dog* came back."

"This doesn't feel like the dog's presence."

The vast, double doors to the old building creak on the hinges as Xander pulls them open. On the other side, the metal door is gouged by scratches, presumably from Syv's dog. The barn is empty and has been for years, rusted farm tools are tossed in a corner amongst old paint tins. I smile at other bottles and cloths arranged on a wooden shelf; looks like Xander does his own car detailing.

I frown and shake my head. "I can detect something, but it might be Spot."

Xander repeats the name derisively and turns to leave. As I follow, I notice something else.

"Xander. Do you guys sleep in here sometimes?"

"Why?"

"I don't know. Like when you argue and want to get away from each other." *Like the big kids you can be.*

He screws up his face. "I had other places and people to escape for a few hours, and it didn't involve cold, dank barns."

I swallow down my jealousy. "I bet you did."

"All of us, Vee, not just me," he says, and I look in surprise as he touches my arm.

I shrug him off. "That's not really relevant right now. Is someone sleeping here?" Walking to a corner, I indicate a screwed-up blanket on the ground on top of a pile of clothes. "Are these from the house?"

Xander crouches down and lifts up the item. "I'm not an expert on what blankets we use, but it could be." He looks at the jeans and then holds up a blue shirt.

"This is Ewan's," I say. "Maybe he hides out in here?"

"Huh." Xander straightens. "If he does, that's bloody weird."

"So these aren't yours from when you're babysitting."

"What?"

"Your baby?" I ask with a smile, then add. "The Aston."

"Very funny." He continues to stare at the items on the floor. "Do they smell of demons?"

"What? I'm not sniffing them!"

"No, can you detect them?"

I shiver, aware we're backed into a corner if somebody walks through the doors. "Nothing here. Let's go."

Xander continues to stare at the items on the floor as we leave, with a troubled look to his brow.

"Xander!" Ewan's voice echoes across the space between us. "Get here, now!"

Without stopping for a breath, Xander charges towards the house. I run to catch up. Ewan stands in the doorway, face pale with Heath beside him.

Xander halts. "What's happened?"

I don't need to ask, because the unmistakable burning scent comes from inside. "Where's Joss?"

Heath rubs his face. "There's a fire. He's trying to grab some books."

"What fire?" demands Xander and strides inside.

"Is it safe?" I ask Heath.

"Contained in the study for now, but with all the books in there..."

"Joss! Out!" calls Xander.

There's an uncomfortable déjà vu to this situation and a fear I'm about to lose the one thing that grounds me: my home. Another fire. Why are we always attacked with fire?

"Xander, no!" I call as he pushes past Ewan and through the door. "You guys aren't fireproof!" No response. "Wait!"

I step forward to follow and Heath seizes my arm. "No. You're not fireproof, either."

I yank my arm away and step back, looking up to the two bedroom windows at the front of the house. No flames yet, but how fast will this spread?

I hold both hands over my face and look to the others as Ewan pulls out his phone.

XANDER

I reach Joss, who stands looking on in shock as the books ignite in the study. The room fills with heat, and I slam the door closed, pulling at his arm.

"Joss. We have to leave, there's nothing we can do and there's a lot of fuel for the fire in there."

"But the books. The one we want to take to the Collector."

"Don't risk it." I tighten my grip, convinced he's about to walk in. We've encountered fires many times, some big, some small, and there's never any way to know how quickly one will take hold. The house's original study door is thicker and heavier than a modern one, maybe giving us a short time to leave before fire bursts through, but not much. The farmhouse still has the wooden-beamed ceilings and some walls are also panelled. The stairs too. Furniture.

A lot of fuel to create a fast fire.

Joss doesn't protest anymore as the thick smoke begins to seep under the door, and we turn to run back out. I halt as I spot a female figure disappearing around the corner and upstairs.

What the fuck, Vee?

Without considering the sudden amount of smoke behind me, or listening to the study door cracking, I throw myself up the steps two at a time.

"Vee! It's too dangerous to grab anything—come on!" I call and then halt in shock as I come face to face with the figure.

Something—or someone—stands in the hallway

between the bedrooms. She's taller than any of the guys, slender and lean. At first, I think her hair is on fire to match the burning eyes, but the flickering doesn't harm her pale skin. We regard each other with silent curiosity, and she extends a hand. With a sweep around her, flames pour from a palm onto the stair rail where they rush down, dancing across the stair carpet and igniting the wood.

What the fuck? I swear I saw Vee.

The woman laughs, a low rumble like thunder sweeping across the hills. As she moves her head, the flames swirl around like snakes. She holds out a hand, palm upright.

"Stone. Then I'll put the fire out." Her accent is strange; she trips over the words as if English isn't her natural language.

"Who sent you? Seth?" I glance back at the smoke billowing on the stairs below.

The woman gestures the length of me. "Burnt body is the end. Ashes." She laughs the same low rumble. "Final."

I swallow. Is the woman right? If something happens because of my stupidity, will Heath be able to put back together a pile of ash?

Fuck. I open the closest bedroom door, run in the room and slam it back closed, heaving in a breath away from the smoke. Before I have a chance to open the window and jump, the door is blasted open, scorched with a space large enough for the woman to walk in.

Spinning, I cross and pull at the window frame, attempting to open it, but the metal glows red and sears my hands. I step back, and for the first time in months, I'm fucking terrified.

I dart a look around the room, weighing up my odds as I back behind the bed. I lean down and turn over the bed, throwing it with force between myself and the woman.

I blink as the flames in her hair spread across her body, like a creature half-way human and half...

Elemental. I've seen creatures like her in Joss's books.

How is she here? The elemental plane is trapped behind a portal; there can't be any of her kind here.

"Where are you from?" I ask as I back up. "How are you here?"

"Give."

"Seriously, you need to expand your vocabulary."

What else can I move? A wooden dresser? Like that's going to be any use. Behind her, flames and smoke follow and there's a crack and crash. Even if the flames were put out now, the house will be gutted.

I pull my shirt up so it covers my nose, a useless barrier against the smoke beginning to fill my lungs. I back up and elbow the window, wincing as the glass breaks and the shards spit across the floor, also landing on my hand.

Fumbling in my pocket, eyes on my attacker, I take the stone and throw it as hard as I can, hoping with every cell that one of the others stands below.

The creature's face darkens, black skin splitting into lines as if fire lies beneath, shining an angry orange. Her eyes glow brighter.

"Stupid Horseman."

"Go get it," I snarl. "Try and take us all on."

"You die. You break the chain. Doesn't matter." The creature lifts a flame-covered hand and blue flames grow in the centre, a more destructive fire.

Is this it? I die at the hands of something I've spent years trying to prevent walking into the world through a portal?

Does Chaos beat me?

Steps thunder up broken stairs and I shout, "Get out! Don't be fucking stupid."

The elemental creature spins around and I recoil as a large canine figure throws itself at her. The woman lands on her back, the dog's weight taking her down as if she were a small child.

Syv's dog.

I cringe, waiting for the creature to burn as the fire engulfs them both, but the dog doesn't flinch as he seizes the woman around the neck. An unearthly scream escapes the creature's lips as the dog's massive teeth tear at her throat, dark blood spilling across the charred skin. The flames flicker around the dog, as if it is made of fire too, and he continues to savage the woman, oblivious to my horror. I cough against the smoke. *Oh great, a hungry hellhound joins the fun.*

The dog releases the limp woman and steps back. The fire surrounding the elemental fades, skin returning to normal colour, making the horrific mess she's become more sickening. Her face is lacerated beyond recognition, flesh hanging from her arms where she's tried to defend herself.

Dead. Am I next?

"I don't have the stone." I snap at the dog as it turns red eyes towards me. "Leave me alone."

He shakes his fur, shaking away the flames as if they're water after a run through a river.

What the fuck is happening here?

As the creature springs forward, launching himself at me, I crouch down, covering my head with my hands. If I die, Heath had better bring me back.

Glass shatters above my head and more showers onto me and the room falls silent. I open an eye. No dog. Someone yells beneath me and the sound is distant because I'm choking to breathe and dizziness is taking over.

I pull myself upwards, ignoring the pain from the sharp

glass in the metal frame. Only jagged edges remain, leaving a space for me to easily jump. If I have the strength.

Of course I fucking do. I'm War.

I heave myself to the edge, and the ground below spins, the four others shouting up at me. Shakily, I climb onto the sill.

The ground comes up to greet me before I have a chance to think what I'm doing.

19

Vee

I sit beside the bed where Xander sleeps beneath a light blue sheet. Soot smudges his face still, but the burns on his hands are gone from where I held them for the last five minutes. Heath stands nearby, arms crossed, as he watches his brother.

"What do you think he'll say when he discovers a hellhound saved him?" he says with an amused quirk to his mouth.

"Demonic dog, please," I say, imitating Syv.

Heath shakes his head, and despite the smile, he can't hide the dark rings below his eyes where he worked with me to help Xander survive.

Help Xander survive. The words were used over and over, and tears pricked my eyes as we tried to rouse him, the muttered 'stupid bastard' lessening as his scorched lungs took him towards death.

He survived. Barely. Xander didn't regain consciousness until after we reached the Collector's, as if something in the flames was stronger than a normal fire and the acrid smoke filling our now-uninhabitable home held a magic poison.

"I can't believe he was so stupid." I've spoken the words so many times that they're worn out, and Heath doesn't reply.

Now we face homelessness as well as the unknown future held in the books. I left Joss staring at the stone and book, with the Collector beside him, but the consternation on his face told me they haven't managed to decipher anything yet. With this many magical beings in one house, I've no idea if anything can get through to attack us.

Breanna contacted Ripley earlier and is working her way back from wherever she went. I understand everybody's suspicions about her and sense Joss's wariness around her the most.

Xander stirs and opens his eyes, sleepy face immediately switching to alert. He outstretches an arm, patting the bed beside him, and when he doesn't find what he wants he springs upright and looks around.

"Where the fuck am I? Where's my knife?"

Something flickers across his face as his memories catch up and he looks at his bare arms. His smooth chest is unscathed too, despite the scorch marks from earlier. How much fire hit him and how much did he breathe in?

Xander coughs and rubs his arms. "I need a shower."

I balk. "Is that all you have to say?"

He pulls back the sheet and stands in his briefs, which is bloody distracting when I'm trying to be angry with him.

"Where are my clothes?" he snaps.

His clothes were torn and scorched, needed removing, and I point to the pile on the floor.

"Pulling my clothes off again, huh, Vee?" he asks.

That's it. My boiling anger bubbles over. "You almost died!" I shout.

"Heath was nearby."

"You almost burned to death!" I continue. "I don't think Heath can reconstruct your body from ash."

"Whoa. Calm down, Vee."

"You have to agree you were bloody stupid, dude," puts in Heath.

I stand and walk to the edge of the room, teeth clenched as I attempt not to lose my temper completely. Or worse, break down in relieved tears. The guys wouldn't let me follow Xander, and Heath held me back. They're right, I don't know how far my powers go, and I could've burned too.

But what if Xander really had been reduced to dust?

"I'll leave you to chat." Heath says quietly, and I hear the door click closed.

I can't hear much above my stressed breathing, so I hold my breath and listen. The bed creaks as Xander sits down, and I turn.

"I thought the elemental was you, Vee."

"Elemental?"

"I saw someone run upstairs and thought it was you following me into the house and checking the bedrooms. Until I came face to face with it." He leans forward and swipes his hand across his hair, then wipes the soot on his trousers. "Then it was too late to use the stairs to get back down."

"Is an elemental a demon?" I ask.

"No. Not quite. There's an elemental plane held behind the portals—a world where everything that lives there can manipulate the elements. This one was obviously a fire elemental. Well, that's what Joss read in one of his books in the past. We've no idea what their world is like."

"A creature from behind a closed portal?" I ask.

Xander's troubled eyes meet mine. "Well, that's the million-dollar question."

"Seth has started opening them?" I whisper. "No. Surely he'd like to make a big deal out of everything and show us."

Xander arches a brow.

"Fuck." I sink onto the bed next to him. "You shouldn't have followed."

He side-eyes me. "I have to look after you, Vee."

"You should know I wouldn't be stupid enough to walk upstairs in a burning building."

"I dunno. Maybe you had something up there you wanted to save."

"More than my life?" I shake my head and shove him in the chest. "I'm fucking furious with you."

Xander holds his hands out and shuffles across the bed, palms outwards. "Okay. Let's leave the 'what Vee does to Xander when she's angry' thing for today. Please."

I open my mouth to retort that I have zero interest in sex, despite the honed magnificence in front of me offering reminders of how bloody good it feels to indulge in him. Then I notice his amused expression. He leans closer and moves hair from my ear, and I shiver as his fingertips brush my chin.

"But I'll be more than happy to oblige later, once I've more energy. We have some unfinished business from the other night, sleepyhead." He finishes his words with a soft kiss, holding the back of my head.

I fight away the immediate response to kiss him back harder, aware what he's doing. I shove Xander in the chest again. "Don't try and get around me like that. I'm pissed off!"

"I want you to understand why I did this, though, Vee. I will always put you first. Always." The earnestness in his green eyes is a million miles from the hardened-eyed expression he'd give me in the early days we knew each other.

"But not by doing idiotic things and almost killing yourself."

He bites his lip and smooths my face with the back of his hand. "It was instinctive, Vee. I was walking up the stairs before I had a chance to think about what I was doing."

I sigh. "Shit. Risking your life isn't a great instinct."

"Yeah. You're telling me."

I'd ask if he regretted what he did, but despite whatever drove him to his insane actions, inside my heart I know Xander would've done this anyway.

He straightens, blinking out of our moment. "The stone. Did someone take it after I threw it down?"

"Yes. Joss and the Collector have them both now."

Xander stands and looks around. "I need some spare clothes. Now. I'm going nuts trying to guess what's happening here. If Seth is sending people after us and threatening the world if we don't bring him the book, everybody is running out of time."

"Yeah. We're all a bit stuck when it comes to clothes," I admit. "The house...it's pretty much destroyed."

Xander's face contorts with anger—and maybe more. His home. His place he always returns. Safe. His anxiety radiates, and I reach out to him. Earlier, I took away his physical pain, and this time I want to give him love and comfort.

I touch his cheek with my fingertips and his expression softens. Our lips touch and he gently holds the back of my head, mouth moving against mine. Soft. Restrained. I rest my forehead on his and we stay like that for a moment in silent understanding. Together, we can all deal with the confusion and hurt surrounding us. We won't be beaten.

Ewan waited around when the fire brigade arrived and tried to save the house. He says there's little left, and the thought sickens me. The guys didn't have much in the world, but what they had was there.

Our world has already burned.

20

HEATH

The door opens and Xander walks in with Joss, who's holding two stones in his hand. How does the Collector feel about his house filled with five refugees?

"How are you now?" he asks Xander.

A freshly showered Xander in jeans and a colourful shirt borrowed from the Collector nods. "I'm fine. Thanks. Do we have what we need now?"

Joss holds the stones tighter. "I think so."

Xander turns to the Collector. "And do you think you can translate this?"

"I think translating will take some time for just one person." The room drops into a tense silence for a moment before the Collector speaks again. "I believe Ripley when he says Breanna can help, and I would wait, but I know you want to find information as soon as possible."

Joss nods. "I'll help. That will speed things up."

"Yes, perhaps one of you can."

One of us? "Shouldn't we all work on this?" I ask. "It'll be quicker."

The Collector shakes his head. "I think too many people will be confusing. And working with people who become frustrated easily won't help."

My mouth twitches into a smile. No guesses who he's talking about. Xander crosses his arms. "Fine. How long will this take?"

"How much do you want to know? I doubt we'll interpret anything but an outline. I don't think we're capable of more."

"I want the outline," Vee puts in. "As soon as you know anything, I need to hear. We all do."

The others voice their agreement.

"I won't be able to sit around waiting," says Ewan. "I want to see if we can salvage anything in the house. Heath? Xander? What about you, Vee?"

She shakes her head. "I'm staying."

Vee looks to Joss, who nods at her. I understand. She shouldn't be in the room when they're trying, because if they misinterpret and Vee hears something terrible, how would she react?

No, we need to wait until Joss has something to share. He leaves us with reassurances he'll tell us everything, as soon as he can, but with trepidation in his eyes.

Joss

I follow the Collector to his study. He sets the book Seth would fight for, and the carved stones, on the table. He rubs his temples as he opens the book and looks from the stones to the symbols scrawled inside.

With apprehension, I sit and we both flick through in silence. I spend an hour comparing the stones, but there's little I can decipher. Tapping my pen on the table, I read over information the Collector passes me for my opinion.

"Please stop. You're annoying me," he says.

I do as he asks, and the Collector sits back dragging hands through his blond curls. "I've lost concentration now!"

"I can take over?" I suggest. "You've a pattern now, haven't you? That should help make out more sentences."

"I'd rather you didn't until what I've found is clearer." He closes the book with his notepad inside. "Have you deciphered any more?"

"I can make out a few words but that's all."

With a sigh he stares down at the book. "I wish Breanna were here. If what Ripley says is true, this would be clearer and quicker."

"Are you saying it's useless us trying to do this?" My stomach leadens. "We can surely find something."

"Yes, we can. But this will take longer."

We return to our work and attempt to put together sentences, or match them to pictures. Chaos and Truth are the most common words, but the Horsemen aren't mentioned as frequently.

I look up at the clock ticking above a nearby fireplace and rub my eyes. Three hours and my head aches with frustration. I never expected this to be easy but, after days chasing around and weeks not knowing who Verity is, we need answers. They're in reach. So close.

But will they be the answers we want?

The Collector interrupts my thoughts. "Joss. I need to talk to you."

"Did you find something?"

I've seen The Collector lose his impassive attitude once, in Portia's presence. Twice now, because he's looking at me as if seeing me through different eyes. He can't hide his thoughts—the Collector doesn't want to tell me what he found.

But he has no choice. He offered to help.

"Yes. I need you to tell me if I've interpreted this correctly." He pushes the notepad across the table, and my hand shakes as I take hold.

21

Joss

The Collector leaves the room, but I can't.

I'm trapped by what we found.

How can I walk through that door, to the barrage of questions, and not cause everybody else's world to fall apart?

They need to know. They will know. But I can't say the words; I can barely repeat them in my head.

Do I speak to Vee first?

Should I explain to her what I've found? Or when we're all together? She gains strength from us being around her. Will that be enough?

I turn back to the text, to our notes, and reread them. This has to be a mistake. This can't be who Vee is.

Isn't everything open to interpretation? A theory? Nobody can see the future.

This doesn't need to happen.
But what if it's the only way?

Vee

I'm half-asleep, the afternoon growing late, and I'm woken by someone walking into the lounge room. The Collector won't look at me and fear seizes my heart. Where's Joss? I watch the door, but he doesn't appear.

"Are the others here?" he asks.

"No. Why?"

I've waited here all day unable to leave. We're aware the storm gathers in the Atlantic as we listen to the news stories about how quickly it moves and how far the devastation could spread.

Seth, showing his might, warning us.

He can destroy us.

He can hurt the world.

And then he can end it.

Seth also sent a message saying he has something special to share, and that if we didn't meet up with him, and bring him answers, he'd begin picking off countries and people one by one.

Does he know we have the stones now?

The Collector glances over and when I catch his eyes, he's forced to approach me. I look back as he takes on his game face, like that of a doctor.

"Where's Joss?" I ask.

"I think he's still reading."

"Did you find anything?"

His face remains impassive, but eyes flicker concern. "Yes."

"What? What did it say?"

He scratches his cheek. "I think we should talk when everybody is here."

I swallow. The other guys need to come back now. I'm surprised they left, but Heath persuaded Xander to walk with him in the nearby park. His pacing and anxiety wasn't helping mine. Ewan hasn't returned from looking over what's left of our house yet.

"Joss will tell me what's happening." I stand and push past him, ignoring the nausea. Why didn't Joss walk straight out too?

The door is closed to the room where Joss sat with the Collector all afternoon, and I hesitate as I close my hand around the smooth metal handle.

Inside, Joss sits with his head in his hands, motionless, quiet. An open book is spread across the table in front of him, beside pens and a notepad covered in scrawled writing.

He looks up as the door clicks closed and when I see the look on his face, I almost turn and run. He's as hollow as the Joss I lost to the wraith.

"Joss?"

He hastily pushes everything into a pile and closes the book, and I walk over and place a hand over his to stop him.

"What did you and the Collector discover?"

"I don't know," he says hoarsely. "I don't know."

"Surely you must've found something. Does it say who I am? Where I'm from?" My mouth dries before I add my biggest question. "Do you know why I'm here?"

He nods and folds his hands beneath his arms, but he can't hide the shaking.

"If you can't tell me, can I read what you've written?"

He glances at the table. "I'm double-checking if this is all correct." I reach out but he stops me, clutching my fingers until they hurt. "Let me tell you what the book says."

"This is bad, isn't it?" I whisper. "How you feel is flooding from you. Is what you've found bad for me, or us?"

He blinks. "Both."

"And for Chaos? Do we stop him? Does this say how?"

Joss lets go of my hands and stands. He turns away, digging hands into his hair and holding his elbows at right angles. For a moment, he's motionless and I watch, stomach churning.

I'm about to ask him again to talk to me when he spins around. I recoil as he swipes everything from the table and swears, shouting, his despair replaced by rage. I'm the most terrified I've been for days. Calm, measured Joss who holds us all together entered this room, and has disappeared leaving this man behind.

I reach out to Joss, but he's lost in whatever grips him. Is he being influenced by something again? Was this the book?

Joss slumps down in his chair and leans forward, head in his hands again, muttering an apology. I approach and wrap my arms around him, instantly feeling the truth.

No, he's just Joss.

"You're scaring me." He looks around as I stroke his face. "Don't hide anything from me."

He nods and strokes hair from my face. "I'm sorry. I should hold things together. That was selfish of me."

"You can't help how you feel."

Joss pulls me onto his lap, the way he's done so many times before, when we sit and chat and joke. When we're

Vee and Joss, sometimes whispering and annoying the others, and being the relaxed 'us' we can be when we help each other unwind.

Only the secrets he whispers now destroy my world in a way Seth never could.

22

Heath

Joss sits next to Vee on the sofa, beating me to the spot, so I sit on the arm on the other side of her. She smiles at me, but her dull eyes betray how much Joss has told her already. I only had minutes to ask questions before he rushed the five of us into the room to talk, and now I know Joss lied when he said only the Collector has answers.

The room drops into a weird silence, and I look between Joss and the Collector, who chooses to sit in his chair. The one he used when we sat here with the betraying bastard, Seth. The day Seth fooled us that he was helping.

"What have you found?" says Xander in a harsh voice. "Everything. Now."

The Collector looks to Joss. "We'll tell you everything we've found so far, Xander. But we haven't translated all the text."

"Fine. Whatever." His voice isn't Xander, and I know mine would waver too.

"Okay. We all agree that Vee contains energy unlike anything seen before." Xander gives a curt nod to the Collector's words. "It is true, Truth has been created to deal with Chaos, but we can't decipher how long ago she became what she is."

"Only a few months," replies Ewan.

"No. Before she was hidden," says Joss. "We think her energy has been in the world for years, passed between uh..." He pauses. "'Vessels' is the word the book used."

I frown. "Put here by who?"

"We're still figuring that out."

Ewan sinks back. "I don't know if I can cope with only knowing some of this."

"Isn't something better than nothing, though?" asks Joss. "We need a head start in case Seth does gather some intel too."

Xander takes a deep breath. "I agree. Carry on."

The Collector pulls the book from his pocket and sets it on the table. He points at a page. "These three words are repeated in the book. Chaos. Order. Truth. We know what that means today, but to other people they are just words, not entities. This suggests Truth and Order have been in the world since the text was written, as well as Chaos."

"So the demon element? They've always existed?"

The Collector shrugs. "Perhaps, but the word Order has many meanings."

"So what? How are the three connected?" I ask.

Joss takes Vee's hand, and for the first time in days a jealousy stabs deep inside. He told her, and they have a deeper bond because of this. "In this text, Truth can bring the end of Chaos," he says.

"And the Order?" asks Ewan. "Does she end them?"

"That's not clear."

"So Vee is here to help us and kill Chaos?" Xander sits forward. "We were right."

"No, Vee is here to close the portals," says the Collector.

I frown. "They are closed. You mean to keep them closed?"

"Yeah, that's our role. What's so different about Vee?" puts in Ewan.

"Maybe close is the wrong word." The Collector exchanges a look with Joss. "End the portals is perhaps a better phrase?"

Joss shifts in his seat and squeezes Vee's hand tighter. She smiles down at him.

Okay. *Now* I'm pissed off he never spoke to me.

"The Horsemen *protect* portals," replies the Collector. "You can't close them permanently, not even together, but you've kept them safe for when Chaos and Truth arrive."

"Oh man, this is confusing," I mutter and my heart beats faster.

The Collector smiles sympathetically. "Joss and I can't yet figure out everything, like we said. I will keep working on this. Breanna can help once she returns."

"Go on," urges Xander.

"The portals needed protecting until the biggest threat to them arrived, and it appears the Horsemen were created with individual powers to take that role."

"By who?" asks Xander sharply.

"Something else we need to figure out." Joss's voice is soft and hesitant. "Sorry."

"Wait," says Ewan. "We figured out that Truth needed us in order to become stronger. So, are you saying she has a bigger power that needs boosting by us or whatever once the time arrives?"

"Yes. Which is what we did, I presume?" asks Xander. "So she contains more than just a combination of our powers?"

The Collector points to the book. "Chaos and Truth are prophesied, in the book. Chaos has to be destroyed when he returns. By joining with the Four Horsemen, Truth is able to do this."

Xander wipes both hands from his face into his hair. "I'm getting lost here. Is Truth a Horseman or not?"

"Key," says Vee.

"What key?" asks Ewan.

"Me. I'm the key. I can open the portals or lock them."

"Then what are *we*?" asks Ewan, face flushing with frustration. "This isn't anything we believed from reading other books."

"Guardians," says the Collector.

Ewan huffs. "Of the portals? Yes."

"No, of the key."

His voice rises. "But we only just found Vee! How can the Horsemen have spent years being guardians of something—someone—we only just met?"

The Collector moves his hand to indicate Ewan should calm down. "We'll figure this out."

Xander stands. "Figure it out?" he half shouts, and I straighten as a familiar switch flicks and his anger grows. "Stop being fucking cryptic! Vee—a key, or whatever. Us, guardians of her —Truth. What? Is she here to kill Chaos? Or close portals he opens? Or both? How does she do all this?"

Joss takes a deep breath. "Chaos created the portals when he was having 'fun'. Looks like someone created us to keep them closed until he could be destroyed. Remember Seth said he's been away—who knows how long for?"

The Collector interrupts. "Now Chaos is back and Truth has her purpose. That's why you had to find her before he did, and to form a bond strong enough to keep you together until she was ready. Truth will destroy the portals and any chance his chaos could enter again, but only if Seth dies."

"Right. So she's here, and we help? Good. That's what I thought." Xander breaks into a relieved smile.

Something's off, because Vee and Joss definitely aren't sharing his relief.

"Death." We all look at Vee, who speaks in a quavering voice then stands and wraps her arms around herself.

I dizzy as I point to the book. "You mean me, right? The other Horsemen are mentioned in the book?"

Vee shakes her head. "No. Seth was right. I'm going to die."

The world stops. A freeze-frame, like the moment before an explosion blasts through a movie scene. But this isn't a movie. This is a fucking nightmare. My ears ring as Vee's words blacken the exploding world for a moment. I don't look at her. At the others. At anything. I attempt to change her words in my mind, to find a different definition.

There's none.

I wait for somebody to react and I shake my head at the Collector. "That's not true."

The Collector's silence pushes my heart rate and suspicion upwards, before he speaks.

"Joss is correct. This will kill her."

Joss swallows and Vee turns her face so we can't see her reaction. Nothing I see or hear makes me sick. Ever. I might panic, or lose my shit sometimes, but I'm never nauseated by anything. But right now, I could heave the contents of my stomach onto the floor in the spinning room.

No.

Fuck, no. They're wrong. My mind repeats the words, reassuring me with denial.

Something Xander shares.

"Bullshit!" he shouts. "Total bullshit! I don't know what you read, but you need to look again! Vee is not going to die. You said she's powerful—more powerful than Chaos—nobody can kill her. Chaos can't kill her."

"Chaos won't kill me, Xander." Vee clears her throat, finding the voice we can barely hear. "I need to release the power we've created. That's what kills me."

Xander's stunned into silence, and I glance at Ewan, whose shock matches. This was supposed to be a battle—kill or be killed—and we were going to win. This isn't supposed to be this way.

I turn to her. "No. The Collector just said it. You kill Chaos and close the portals. You have to live to close them, surely?"

"When I die." Vee clears her throat. "That's when Chaos dies. The energy inside me is linked to him too, and powerful enough to wipe him out and his portals. Truth contains all the power needed; the raw energy has to be unleashed against him."

"How?"

Vee shakes her head and bites on her lip. "I don't know yet."

"Then we all die," says Xander hoarsely. "We fight Chaos with Vee and die with her."

The Collector and Joss exchange another of their bloody annoying, knowing glances. "There's nothing here to say the Horsemen die."

"Of course we fucking do!" he snaps. "We can't live without our Fifth!"

Of everything spoken in the last few minutes, Xander's outburst shocks me the most but his words are chained between all of us, the chain that circles Vee. Not Truth, Vee. He may be saying the Horsemen won't live after she dies, but I hear his other meaning.

How can we be whole if Vee leaves us?

"No," says Ewan. "I think we'll all die. I mean, our existence will be pointless with no portals to protect."

I'm about to protest that Horsemen don't die, but who knows what the fuck counts as mortality in this situation? If our role was to activate Vee, or whatever, we must be surplus to requirements now.

"I want to read your notes ," says Vee in a quiet voice. "I need to know everything."

Ewan breaks his silence. "This is confused prophecy bullshit. We'll figure this out. There must be a way to kill Chaos that doesn't kill Vee."

"What confuses me," says the Collector, "is Chaos must be half-sure Vee's here to take him out, so why hasn't he hit first?"

"Seth told me Vee was stronger than him," mutters Ewan. "When he fought me. She can do this. We can do this. Vee doesn't need to die."

But despite his words, I can tell his belief is shaky.

"At least we have time while Seth figures this out," says Xander.

"Time for what?" I ask.

"Time to find another way to kill Chaos," suggests Heath. "The Horsemen have kept the portals closed for hundreds of years. We can keep doing that. We just need Chaos gone."

The Collector sighs. "Not an option, according to this book."

"Why?" demands Xander.

"Vee's energy kills him and closes the portals. If she doesn't kill him, he opens them and everybody dies anyway. It's not an either-or situation." The Collector runs a hand across his head. "I'm very sorry. I don't know what to say to make this better."

"We appreciate your help." Vee's words sound wrong, as if she's thanking him for a ride home or a mundane task. Not telling her she'll die. "With everything. Helping Syv find the stone, helping us with deciphering and letting us stay. You're very kind."

He nods curtly. "I wish I had better news."

I stare at my hands. Kind? How can she be calm and focus on the Collector? This is a mindfuck. Yes, I expected Vee to have a role that we knew nothing about, but not to destroy a god who could end the world and even the universe by dying herself. That's beyond anything I expected fate to throw at us.

This situation can't happen.

It won't happen.

"It has to happen." As if reading my thoughts, Vee reaches out and places a hand on my leg. Her huge green eyes look back in trepidation but with a weird calm. She looks to Joss and whispers something in his ear.

The look on his face chills my soul, because he's lost.

We all are.

23

Vee

The meeting ends abruptly as Xander leaves, knocking into furniture as he does. Although Joss told me the information before the meeting, hearing everything outlined and the truth shared with everybody important in my life dropped the full weight on my shoulders.

Xander's reaction didn't surprise me, but his words did. I've watched him lose control more and more recently, and I hope this isn't his tipping point. I clung onto Joss as we attempted to hold each other together, but it's hard when I sensed he was losing his control again.

I stumble to my feet and follow Xander, who stands in the hallway, head and palms against the wall. Heath's shock and Ewan's quiet scare me. What will be said next?

"Xander," I say, and touch his shoulder.

He doesn't respond, despite me trying several times to

get his attention. I turn back to the others, eyes filling with tears, but not for myself, because I'm numb. Their pain and anguish flood towards me, and I struggle to breathe through the intensity from all four guys at once.

Ewan steps towards me; I'm squashed against his chest, face smothered as he holds me tight. I gasp against him for breath, unable to move. I don't want to feel him hurting; I can't stand feeling how fractured each of their hearts and minds are. His breath comes fast against my hair, but he doesn't speak. I squeeze my eyes, willing the tears to go, because if he sees them, it will make things worse.

I pull back and Ewan holds my face in both hands, lost eyes searching mine. "We'll fix this, Vee. He won't win."

I nod and loosen his hands from my face, watching for Heath's reaction. He hasn't said a word; barely spoke in our meeting. His head's bowed, fringe in his face obscuring his eyes the way he likes to hide sometimes. I cross to him and hold my palm against his cheek.

"Heath." He doesn't look up. "Don't you shut me out too."

"Let me hold this together," he whispers. "Don't let me break down. Not now. If one of us does, we all will."

My heart tears, pulled between the four of them, our bond's intensity pulling our souls apart too. The cruelty stuns me. Whatever the hell we are, underneath we're people with human emotions.

I look to the ceiling and hold back the desire to scream at the universe for hurting the people I love.

Somehow, we find ourselves back in the Collector's room, as he tells us to take time, half-joking that we're crowding his hallway. His attempt to break the tension fails. I sit back on the sofa beside Joss. Xander stands far from the rest of us, arms wrapped tightly around himself. I'd go to him, but if I stand my legs will shake, and if Xander pushes me away again, he'll trigger what I'm holding back—that I want to curl up in a ball and cry.

"We head back to the house," he says after several quiet minutes.

"We can't, Xander," Joss replies. "There's nothing left, remember?"

He spins around ready to retort and I watch as realisation crosses his defeated face. "Oh. Yeah."

"Where do we go?" asks Heath. "We're homeless now."

"The Collector says we can stay here," Joss says. "Though I get the impression he wants this short term."

"No. Maybe a night, but then we move on. Seth's succeeded in smoking us out—literally—so now we go to the bastard." Xander grabs his jacket. "I still want to see what's left of the house, maybe we can salvage something."

I exchange glances with Heath. Ewan said there was little left. But if Xander needs to do this, it could help matters.

"Besides, my car is there," he grumbles.

"Are you thinking about your fucking car now?" Ewan interrupts, incredulous voice loud. "After what we've just been told, you're worried about that?"

Xander narrows his eyes at Ewan. "No."

Joss grabs Ewan's sleeve as he stands. "I think he's trying to deflect how he feels, Ewan."

"What are you? My fucking psychologist now?" shouts Xander.

"We need to discuss and get our heads around what we've just discovered," Joss continues. "Overreacting won't help!"

Ewan drags his sleeve away. "Overreacting? Someone just told us Vee was going to die and there's nothing we can do to stop it."

I cringe back in the seat. What hurts me more, talk of my death or the division happening in the room?

"Bullshit," snarls Xander. "Prophecies are *bullshit*."

I watch the exchange around me, heart racing so hard I start to lose my breath.

Joss grips my hand; his presence helps. But with the numbing horror comes a relief—relief that I finally know the truth about myself.

Will I die? Can we stop this?

"Vee?"

I shake my head, unable to speak, frightened I'll inflame the situation somehow. I'll stop Chaos. I don't know what will happen to me, but the power Logan sees—that I feel—inside me will explode one way or another.

But what if the devastation I saw in my vision the night with Ewan wasn't caused by Chaos, but by me? That in order to kill Chaos, I destroy what's around us?

I blink the thought away. No. I'm here to prevent that.

But still so much remains unanswered, and the lack of firm answers is what gives me hope.

24

*V*EE

The farmhouse should bring familiarity but is devoid of everything we had. The people who return are carrying heavier burdens than when they left and have nothing to return to.

"Is it safe to enter?" I ask as we stare at the building. From the outside, there's little difference, the front of the building intact. I look up to the broken window Xander jumped through and my pulse picks up at the memory.

We step inside, to a different place than the one we left. The walls are covered in black, the stairs missing. Some furniture is half-burnt and the rest gone. The guys, as usual, don't care about minor things like safety. Joss picks his way across the blackened floor until he reaches the kitchen. The room is gutted, everything inside unrecognisable.

"I should've put the fire out in the study the moment I saw it." Joss moves to stand in where the doorway once was, and his upset reaches me. Everything. Gone. All the books, all the notes. All he uses to research and help.

The acrid smell inside the house's shell sticks to my clothes and I hold my hand across my nose, not wanting to breathe anything in. Heath joins us and we all stare helplessly at the room. I don't want to see anywhere else.

"Where did Xander go?" I ask. "He hasn't tried to go upstairs, I hope."

"No. There's no way up there anymore. The rooms are burnt out."

"I'm guessing you didn't have an insurance policy," I say with a small smile.

Ewan blinks at me. "Why are you flippant? This is a huge problem!"

"You think?" I snap back.

"Guys..." Joss touches both our arms. "At least we all survived."

"What was the dog doing here?" I ask.

"Why did he run into a burning building is the bigger question," replies Heath. "And when he ran, he was unscathed."

"Perhaps hellhounds hate elementals?" suggests Heath.

"Perhaps it doesn't matter, just that he saved Xander."

I chew my lip. I'm relieved the conversation has switched from me, but I can't stay in here. "I'm headed outside."

The way across the kitchen involves picking through broken items and twisted metal. How intense was this fire? Outside, Xander sits on the wooden bench, the place we occasionally go to clear our heads when the weather allows.

He looks up as I approach. "I never found anything around the grounds or house. I thought Seth might've left us a message, as he always likes to."

"We're sure it's Seth who sent the elemental?"

Xander looks in confusion. "Um. Yeah. Haven't you noticed how much fire is used against us?"

"True." I sit next to Xander and take his hand. "Everything will be alright."

He stares ahead. "I should be the one reassuring you."

"You need to process this."

"How can you be so calm?" He still doesn't look at me, but his clammy hand tightens against mine.

"Because we haven't lost yet. And there won't be a yet. I agree, prophecies are bullshit." He turns to see my weak smile, but I only half-believe what I'm saying.

The other three guys appear and we gather around each other in the bleak weather. "We need to find the where and when," says Joss. "We need to know everything we can find in that book."

"I think even if he causes storms and opens all the portals, that's not enough to cause the devastation he wants," replies Heath. "Yes, it will fuck up the world and lead to a lot of human death, but Chaos wants to actually destroy everything."

Xander stands. "I'm not having the fucker think he's beaten us and won the first round by destroying a house. He hasn't destroyed us, and he's tried long enough. Despite everything, we know more than him. We regroup, and we track him. I don't know how, but we will."

"Then what?"

Xander looks ahead and says in a quiet voice. "When we're ready, we end this."

The house may be gone, along with everything the guys own, but more than our house has been destroyed in recent days. The undercurrent of distrust, and the need to hide secrets from each other left with him. The only thing that can help now is total unity.

Xander's right. We will win.

But something stirs in the pit of my stomach. The strange sensation that I fought in the past—the one wanting me to end my emotional connection to the guys and the world.

The part of me designed to end Chaos, and now, myself.

25

Vee

Ironically, I return to my burnt flat too, ending my time living here where I began. I'm the only one with possessions left to take with us, wherever we decide to go next.

The landlord tried to contact me a few times about everything I left here; his insurance company want to begin repairs. Luckily, the fire here was minor compared to what I witnessed yesterday, and I have more to salvage since my initial move to the guys' place was a hastily packed bag.

I rummage through the boxes someone placed my possessions in, unsure if I want any reminders of that life. Most of my clothes also stink of smoke, but I've no option. At least I have more clothing choice than the guys do now.

"Do you want me to take your stuff and stash it at the Collector's?" asks Heath. "He offered."

I chew my lip as I pick out a few items of clothes and shove them in a backpack. "I guess. The landlord said he'd dump everything if I didn't collect the boxes by the end of the week."

Heath nods and crouches down to take a large box. "Finish up. I'll take them to the car."

Today feels oddly like the last time I moved from my flat. If everything was screwed up then, now it's a hundred times worse. Where do we go now? I can't see us staying at the Collector's more than a day or two before Xander moves us on. We've discussed heading to the States and are prepared to take a step closer to Seth. Maybe that's what Seth wants, but he'll have a bigger fight on his hands then he expects.

As I stand in my old bedroom, I run a hand through my hair and look around. The curtains are burnt rags, and there's a scorched trail across the carpet. Oddly, my bed and dresser survived, as if the fae who attacked me focused the damage on pushing me from the room. Why didn't it spread?

I open a dresser drawer and peek inside, but the contents must be in one of the boxes. There's a soft tap on the half-open door, and I turn to see Heath standing, hands in pockets.

"Everything okay?"

I shake my head. "No. I'm struggling to hold myself together right now, but I don't want to tell everybody."

He steps in, before closing the door behind him. "You mean you don't want to tell Xander and Ewan?"

As I expected, they're the two not dealing by using denial, and that's holding them together. How long can the pair keep the denial going? Xander's comes through in outbursts, but I worry about Ewan.

As Heath pushes hair from his face with both hands, he looks, eyes filled with a sense of sadness that's worse than when I see them worried.

"Heath, it's okay. I'll be okay."

"I can stop this," he says and strides over.

I gasp as Heath catches me in his arms and hugs me to him. He holds me tightly as if I might disappear, the way he did the first day I arrived in their lives, outside the house when I almost ran.

"I can bring the others back. If you die, I'll bring you back." His hand moves to the back of my head and presses my face against his shoulder. Heath's heart races faster than I've ever heard.

"We can try," I whisper.

Heath tips my face so I can look him in the eyes. "We have to believe we can. That I can."

I don't want to say the question that instantly fills my mind: what if Seth kills Heath first?

"I don't want to talk about dying, Heath."

Instead, I push my mouth on his, desperate for the comfort he can provide. We kiss as if this is the first and last time, gripping each other as our hearts pull together terrified they'll be broken and lost. I'm lost to him and to focusing on the Heath who I wanted from the beginning; on the man who, in a small way, connects me to my old life.

I pull away. "Remember the first time? When I said I wanted to be Vee and be human?"

He plays his fingers across my cheeks and lips, nodding as our eyes meet again in a memory of that night.

"Right now, do I feel less human than that day?"

Heath laughs softly. "You know you feel a hundred percent human to me. Maybe this power can be let go instead of...." He pauses and swallows. "Then you can go back to being just Vee?"

I close my eyes. "Heath, I never was just Vee, was I?"

He steps back and pinches the bridge of his nose. "You know what? I want to destroy whoever made you into this as much as I want to end that fucking god."

"But if they hadn't created me, I wouldn't exist."

That's one truth we can't deny. Heath sits on the bed, and I sit on his lap, arms around his neck. Lying his head against my chest, Heath circles the small of my back with his fingers. I am human. Whoever did this created someone who could feel all the human emotions—the ability to love, desire, hurt, hate... everything. If I was just a power sent to end a god, why give me this?

But as I hold Heath, I know why. The intensity of my need to hold and be held by him, to be with and share love with the four guys, shows they made a mistake. Perhaps my creator decided an emotional connection would help Truth walk in and steal all the Horsemen's powers.

Wrong. Their plans will backfire. We've been through a lot dealing with Chaos and building our strength as the Horsemen and their Fifth—but also as Vee, Ewan, Xander, Heath and Joss.

We won't be beaten easily, prophecy or not.

"You know what I'm going to ask now?" I whisper against his stubbled cheek, as the hurt inside is replaced by something else.

"You never need to ask, Vee. Just tell me what you want. Always."

"To feel the human Vee, like our first time." He nods in understanding, and as we kiss again, the tears build. I'm thankful Heath can't see, but I'm grateful they do because they mean I'm more than any prophecy tells us.

The book talks of Chaos, Truth and Order. But what about Love?

To be continued

OTHER BOOKS BY LJ SWALLOW

The Four Horsemen Series
Reverse Harem Urban Fantasy
Legacy
Bound
Hunted
Guardians
Chaos
Descent
Reckoning

The Soul Ties series
New Adult Paranormal Romance/Urban Fantasy
Fated Souls: A Prequel Novella
Soul Ties
Torn Souls
Shattered Souls

ABOUT THE AUTHOR

LJ Swallow is a USA Today bestselling paranormal romance and urban fantasy author who is the alter-ego of bestselling contemporary romance author Lisa Swallow.

Giving in to her dark side, LJ spends time creating worlds filled with supernatural creatures who don't fit the norm, and heroines who are more likely to kick ass than sit on theirs.

For more information:
ljswallow.com
lisa@lisaswallow.net

facebook.com/ljswallowauthor

twitter.com/lisa_swallow_au

Printed in Great Britain
by Amazon